APPARITIONS

First published by Charco Press 2025
Charco Press Ltd., Office 59, 44-46 Morningside Road, Edinburgh
EH10 4BF

Copyright © Margo Glantz 1996
in agreement with Puentes Agency
First published in Spanish as *Apariciones* (Mexico City: Alfaguara)
English translation copyright © Ellen Jones 2026

The rights of Margo Glantz to be identified as the author of this work
and of Ellen Jones to be identified as the translator of this work have
been asserted by them in accordance with the Copyright,
Designs and Patents Act 1988.

All rights reserved. This book is copyright material and must not be copied,
reproduced, transferred, distributed, leased, licensed or publicly performed
or used in any way except as specifically permitted in writing by the
publisher, as allowed under the terms and conditions under which it was
purchased or as strictly permitted by the applicable copyright law.
Any unauthorised distribution or use of this text may be a direct
infringement of the author's and publisher's rights, and those
responsible may be liable in law accordingly.

A CIP catalogue record for this book is available from the British Library.

Print ISBN: 9781917260183
Ebook ISBN: 9781917260190

www.charcopress.com

Edited by Fionn Petch
Cover design by Pablo Font
Typeset by Laura Jones-Rivera
Proofread by Fiona Mackintosh

EU GPSR Authorised Representative
LOGOS EUROPE, 9 rue Nicolas Poussin, 17000,
LA ROCHELLE, France
E-mail: Contact@logoseurope.eu

2 4 6 8 10 9 7 5 3 1

Margo Glantz

APPARITIONS

Translated by
Ellen Jones

CONTENTS

The Sirens of the World	1
He Approaches	2
The Revelation	3
You Close Your Eyes	3
Naming Her	4
The Woman's Story	4
The Red Pyjamas	5
You Watch Them	6
A Severe-Looking Dress	7
Open-Palmed	7
She Is Wearing a White Shirt	8
Your First and Middle Fingers	8
Ghosts	9
It Is Time	10
Are You Coming?	11
Looking Towards the Horizon	11
I Have Named Her Now	12
Orthopaedic Lessons	13
A Mortal Husband	13
Modesty	14
Are They Visions?	15
She Keeps Time	16
A Gold Ring as a Symbol	17
Rules of Behaviour	18
She Is Gracious, Pure, Exacting	19

Tropical Music	21
You Know Exactly Who He Is	21
A Long Black Silk Gown	22
She Is Cold	23
Distinguishing Features	23
Temperance	24
Your Reading Material	25
The Places of the Heart	26
From the Balcony You Can See the Street	26
She Despairs	27
In the Foetal Position	28
Her Eyes Reveal a Desire	29
The Black Veil	29
A Full, Red Skirt	31
She Is Quiet a Long Time	31
Delicious Pain	32
The Bed of Thistles	32
It Damages the Spine	33
You Catch Him Looking	33
The Eyes of Her Body	34
Stealthily	36
Encounters	36
A Strange White Efflorescence	37
Men Ride Astride Their Horses	37
Did You Hear Her?	38
Exemplary Behaviour	39
The People's Abode	40
Her Trousers Are Blue	40
A Faint Smell of Manure	41
The Sin of Pride	42

The Path from the Mouth to the Heart	42
Strange Apparitions	43
Scratches	44
The Soul Is Inebriated	45
One Note at a Time	46
Fingers and Marks	48
Continuous Movement	48
She Behaves Badly	51
The White Roses	51
Simple Words	52
He Commiserates with Her Sorrow	53
On the Edge of the Bed	54
Love of My Life!	55
You Are Astonished	56
His Head Is Leaning	56
Tense Hands	57
You Raise Your Arms	57
She Strips to the Waist	58
Captivated	59
Submitted to a Desire	60
The Gaunt Body	60
Food Is Seasoned	61
Spiritual Exercises	61
The Voices of the Nunnery	62
The Beauty of Her Eyes	63
The Areola Is Pink	64
In Distress	64
Cupid or Archangel?	65
I Take Off My Shoes	66
A Wall	66

Carelessness	67
Wool Against Silk	67
An Unlikely Position	68
Tears and Sighs	68
Discordant Voices	69
Pictorial Copies	70
Like Dogs	71
You Tremble	72
The Hair Shirt	73
You Weep	74
She Glances In	75
His Shape Has Changed	75
A Faint Thread of a Voice	76
Lamb of God	77
Delicately	78
They Do Not Need Food	79
Her Greedy Thirst	79
A Certain Cadence	80
The Shadow of His Mouth	81
You Would Like to Do Her Make Up	84
The Girl Tells You	85
The Dirty, Dark Red Mouth	86
She Falls	87
Face Up	89
She Looks at Herself in the Mirror	89
The Brush of His Hand	90
A Spark	91
The Heavily Made-Up Face	92
If There Is Love	93
Everything Is Clearer	93

From One Mouth to the Other	94
Very Suddenly	95
The Visions	96
Rings on Your Fingers	97
My Only Torment	98
The Players	99
The Same Cry	101
The Wedding	101
Miracle of Miracles	104
Acknowledgments	107

To Sergio Pitol, with enormous affection and gratitude

*To Beatriz Aguad, Luz del Amo and Diamela Eltit,
in alphabetical order and with great fondness*

THE SIRENS OF THE WORLD

I begin by saying:
When I write, I am perhaps someone called Lugarda Aldana de Villarroel —or am I Juana de Soto y Guzmán?—
(out in the world),
later I am Sister Lugarda de la Encarnación —or Sister Teresa Juana de Cristo?—
(in the convent),
and so I say:
—I ask of you, father, if you care anything for me, that you consider my salvation. Let not your daughter remain so long exposed to the sirens of the world. If you had promised me to a mortal husband in a distant land, you would never have seen me again. And yet it angers you that we are separated by mere walls because I wish to bind myself to a heavenly husband.
And she who speaks within my text pauses and then begins again, more forcefully:
—Why do you hold me against my will? Why do you begrudge me a tiny cell and a humble table in the family of Christ?
I shall pause my tale here, ready to resume it at a more favourable moment.

HE APPROACHES

You see him approach, moving with long, quick strides. He's coming over, pushing the door.

I get your attention, warn you, asking:

Why are you trembling?

You are silent.

But he is already close. He approaches and says:

—Take off your clothes.

You do so.

You are now naked.

—On the floor! he orders.

You obey.

—Not like that, he repeats, on all fours!

You get down on all fours. He looks at you, undresses, and slowly mounts you.

He enters you.

Once again he says, softly, decisively:

—Move!

And you move.

He slaps your hips. You tremble, and say: go on, go on, more, more!

He obeys, moving inside you, slapping you.

—Did you come?

—Yes, you reply.

THE REVELATION

I am writing again. I come, and I write her.
I am dressed soberly. I place my fingertips humbly on the keyboard, soft, cosy, intimate. Writing soothes me, soothes the anxiety of waiting.

Writing is a spell. Especially when I have my revelation, when I figure out what name to give her:
   —*They call her Sister Lugarda de la Encarnación now. Out in the world she went by the name of Lugarda Aldana Torres de Villarroel.*

YOU CLOSE YOUR EYES

—Are you coming?
—Yes, you say, I'm coming.
And you add:
—Can't you tell I'm coming?
I add, harshly:
—Can't you see it's not the same? It's not the same when you lie face down, fully dressed, and start licking the bones someone tossed on the floor, as when you undress, get down on all fours, follow his orders, rump in the air like a dog, and wait for him to mount you.
You look at me questioningly:
—That's why, I go on, he slaps you on the flanks, so you'll obey him, move, look up, close your eyes, open your mouth, and be left spent, frozen in a pained grimace.
—Did you come?

You do not reply, but turn to him and ask:
—Have you come yet?

NAMING HER

I won't give up, I insist, I'll keep writing.

I tell myself I must decide, that I have to give her a name, yes, I have to name the woman. Although some time ago, before giving her a name, I had written:

'Her seclusion and strict cloistering has been admirable, for the modesty she showed long before becoming a nun was clear proof of her extraordinary nature, of her constancy and strength which, later, once she was wed to Christ, the Blessed Sacrament, her sweet, dead husband, gave her eyes for him alone.'

THE WOMAN'S STORY

You are alone.
 I go over.
 I ask:
 —Why did you like the painting so much?
 You reply:
 —The one I saw in the museum with him?
 —Yes, I say, you seem to love it.
 You pause. You are thinking.
 Finally, you reply:
 —I like the painting, but mainly I like the story of the woman, I like the story of her disappearances. That ability she had, to be there and not be there at the same

time, the gift of ubiquity, of occupying and vacating a space and always being present although hidden, like Christ, or like the girl.

THE RED PYJAMAS

The girl is in the bedroom. She is asleep in red pyjamas, an all-in-one, the type that undoes between the legs.

Once certain she is asleep, he says:

—Come, stand up.

He takes you to a corner of the room and leans you against a column.

—Raise your arms, he orders.

You raise them, your armpits curly, light brown in colour.

He undresses you gradually as you continue to lean on the column, and you let him, your arms raised. And when he enters you, you feel a slight pain, your legs slightly spread so you can keep your balance, but then you lift them, wrap them around his waist so he can move comfortably inside you, and lower your arms.

—Lift them up! he repeats, quietly, unequivocal.

Once you obey, you are at his mercy. Your balance is precarious as he moves, which inhibits you a little. You follow his rocking motion cautiously because you are convinced you will fall otherwise, but still, you close your eyes, raise your arms and derive some pleasure from his rhythm.

Something unsettles you. You open your eyes, look over to the bed and see her sitting in her red pyjamas watching you in surprise; he has seen her too. He goes on moving without paying her any attention, seemingly unbothered, ordering you to close your eyes and raise your arms again.

You obey.

The girl's gaze bores into you, turning you on, turning him on even more, until you both reach orgasm and are left spent, one on top of the other. You are floored, your arms limp by your thighs.

The girl's look electrifies you.

YOU WATCH THEM

You lean out over the balcony and look down. You watch them, watch them making love, watching the dogs making love to each other, watch carefully how the male approaches the female, how he sniffs her, licks her, plays with her, mounts her, rides her, panting, how she pants too, in turn. You watch them in fascination, the colours of their fur intermingled, hers light, his reddish-brown, both silky, fluffy. They grow still, completely immersed in one another.

A long time later the male gets off the female, goes over to the wall and urinates, his penis a long red dripping string of gut.

You close the window, go into your room, stand in front of the mirror, undress, kneel down, masturbate, look up at your reflection in the mirror and see light in your eyes.

—Did you come?

A SEVERE-LOOKING DRESS

I say, say to myself, tell myself:
—Write!
And I obey my own command:
I sit down at the machine wearing a severe-looking dress printed with classic, small, dark grey images, delicate symmetrical figures in shades of beige and white. It's ankle length, and covers my arms, my chest.
I start writing. I write.
I tell myself I have to give her a name:
—That's it, she will be called Juana Teresa de Cristo. Though isn't Lugarda de la Encarnación a better name?

OPEN-PALMED

He turns round and you are sitting with your legs pressed together like a girl brought up in a convent.

—Take off your clothes! he orders.

Now you are naked.

He looks at you, runs his gaze over your entire body. You stand before him, whole, your nipples erect. A shiver runs through you and you feel yourself getting wet.

He orders you again:

—Get down on all fours!

And when you do, he mounts you. He slaps your flanks rhythmically, open-palmed, moving inside you.

You follow his every movement precisely: you know how to obey.

Suddenly he asks, still inside you:

—Would it turn you on more if the girl were watching?

You are silent for a while, then you repeat what you have said before:
—Love that begins like lava ends up barren.

SHE IS WEARING A WHITE SHIRT

He has told you before, while looking at the girl. She is lying on the sofa wearing blue jeans and a white top, her legs spread. He told you, looking at her and looking at you:
—Girls should sit with their knees together or their legs crossed.
You look at her again, and then at him. You look at him in surprise. The girl, impassive, spreads her legs even wider.

YOUR FIRST AND MIDDLE FINGERS

You don't know why, but an intense memory now comes to mind: you remember the first months of the girl's life. She cried a lot, and you, affected, cried with her, letting your tears fall on her little face. Your tears mixed together. Then, taking your breast delicately between your first and middle fingers, you nursed her. She would clamp her gums immediately onto your nipple, dark, red, rough and swollen, like your own eyes.

It's her thirst, that's all, that thirst that consumes you.

GHOSTS

That's why you like repeating it, the story of the portrait, that portrait where she appears and disappears like ghosts or like Christ in the nuns' visions. You love the fact that, even though it's just a process of restoration, a laborious and complicated technique, the apparitions are real.

I'm talking about the portrait you saw with him in that museum, the portrait we talked about recently, that portrait exhibited along with the full-size photographs, the ones that show all the modifications the painting has undergone. Her body was covered up by another body, that of a man with a feminine, graceful air. Thanks to the photos, we can see that his body was positioned entirely over the effaced body of the young woman, adopting the same posture she had when she was still in the portrait, riding side-saddle like a lady.

The rider appears to be a man because of his clothing and posture, sitting astride his horse. But he reminds us of a woman, with his enigmatic smile, smooth countenance and rosy cheeks, the voluptuous sway of his hips and head, the twinkle in his eye. We recognise her in the photograph, taken before the painting was restored, and that is how we know, we know the rider is hiding her, we know she is there underneath, despite the layers of paint covering her body, those layers removed one by one, bit by bit, by those who understand the complicated processes of restoration.

In the restored painting, the successive overlays of oil paint removed – layers applied to cover her up in the same way earlier writings on a palimpsest are covered – she is wearing a red riding suit and her gaze is surprisingly reminiscent of the girl when she looks at your lover. Neither of them wears make-up and both have a gleam in their eye.

IT IS TIME

So I say to myself again:
—It's time for you to write, now.
And I do.

My skirt is velvet with a silky, pearl grey lining and I have finely striped tights to match; my shoes, special shoes, which are only for writing, are green in colour, a steely green made of fine leather; the medium height heels are delicately shaped and have a slight incline that allows me to plant my feet firmly on the ground, to write comfortably, without tiring.

I undress myself from the waist up. Before writing I like to stroke my nipples. They are rough, and the touch excites me, I twist them in my fingers one by one, alternating, wanting them to go red, erect, shiny, hot. I run my fingertips over the areola until they too are thrumming, and in that sense of exaltation I prepare myself.

I place my fingers on the keyboard.

—Write! I tell myself again, when I realise I have stopped writing, too focused on the ritual of preparing myself for writing.

And I answer myself:

—I am writing.

And then I really do write.

—I'm writing her, I say out loud as I mark the letters on the keyboard. She has taken the name of Sister Lugarda de la Encarnación, or perhaps of Sister Teresa Juana de Cristo, and I add, to finish:

—Writing and sexuality are always exercised in private spaces and for that very reason are susceptible to violation. Yes, secret spaces, spaces where mortal risk is run.

ARE YOU COMING?

Gradually, almost without realising, you have become his prey. You can no longer pretend otherwise to yourself.

He is still on top of you, riding you furiously, and you move furiously too as he takes your nipples, pulls them, pinches them, squeezes them.

You come, then, like a dog, on all fours, burning, wet, your nipples hot.

He murmurs hot words in your ear and you tremble.

—Move! he says again, slapping your flanks.

And you move. Exhausted, he leans on you, covering you as though you were a mare, and then again, gathering momentum, he rides you, pulls out and pushes into you again, wet. His milk lubricates you, your labia drink it in, your rump in the air like a dog.

—Did you come? I ask.

—Yes, you answer, hard.

LOOKING TOWARDS
THE HORIZON

—I think, I say to you, that the custom of painting people's portraits standing by a window was deeply rooted in the ancients. It's a custom that the moderns, with a few rare exceptions, have not yet fully understood.

You look at me strangely. You have no idea what I'm talking about.

—I'm referring, I explain, to that portrait we're always mentioning, the portrait you and he saw together, the portrait of the disappearances.

—I still don't understand, you reply.

—I think that if they had put her next to the window, that is, looking towards the horizon, as well as allowing us to see the figure more completely, it would have added something highly lyrical and suggestive. The fragment of the figure we can see puts the mind to work in such a way that a feeling of surprise and discovery soon intervenes: anyone looking at the portrait ends up wondering what might be behind the wall where the window ends.

—Who are you referring to, the girl?

—Yes, her.

—You talk in riddles. The only thing that seems likely to me is that if she had disappeared from the portrait she would have hidden behind the window to spy on us. Isn't that the kind of thing she would do? You should know, seeing as you spy and give out orders, too, don't you? Aren't you my perfect double?

You stop, reflect, and add in conclusion:

—Something that speaks of loss, of destruction, of the disappearance of things, doesn't speak of itself, it speaks of others. Will it include them too?

I HAVE NAMED HER NOW

I am sad. I look at myself in the mirror, feeling sorry for myself. And to avoid this, I write. I know that doing so calms me. That is why I do it.

I do it reluctantly, with barely the strength to write a few phrases. This is understandable. Simply by naming her, I will know who I am.

I have named her now, I have called her Sister Lugarda de la Encarnación.

I come while I'm writing.

ORTHOPAEDIC LESSONS

He tells you again:
—Get down on the floor.
This time you refuse.
He warns:
—I like having you down on the floor like a dog, the pleasure is much more intense when you're on all fours.
At that moment you remember the orthopaedic lessons:
'By standing erect, man has usurped a place in the world that does not belong to him. He should move as mammals do, with four feet on the ground, and make love like horses and dogs, the female below, the male on top, embracing her with his hind legs: the ancient position of Pasiphae and the bull.'

A MORTAL HUSBAND

When I write, my feet placed firmly on the floor, I could be Lugarda Aldana de Villarroel —or Juana de Soto y Guzmán? — (out in the world),

and later Sister Lugarda de la Encarnación —or Sister Teresa Juana de Cristo?—(in the convent).

Using my words, the ones I am writing now, the words I like to repeat, I say:

—I ask of you, father, if you care anything for me, that you consider my salvation. Do not let your daughter remain so long exposed to the sirens of the world. If you had promised me to a mortal husband in a distant land, you would never have seen me again. And yet it angers you that we are separated by mere

walls because I wish to bind myself to a heavenly husband. Why do you hold me against my will? Why do you begrudge me a tiny cell and a humble table in the family of Christ?

I write, now that I have escaped that siege of words cut short, now that I can give them timbre, density, their true register, height and colour.

I write and I say:

Today, Juana de Soto y Guzmán —or is she Lugarda Aldana de Villaroel?— takes her vows.

MODESTY

You sit on the sofa next to the girl. She has her legs spread and is wearing blue trousers and a white shirt.

Standing before you both, he explains to her:

—Women should always appear modest, no matter where they are. This is achieved by remaining composed and controlling the gaze. A careless gait and excessive movement of the hands or any other part of the body lead only to the loss of dignity: they are manifest signs of frivolity. That is why girls and young women should make sure their face, demeanour and gestures are decent, that nothing interferes with the natural colour of their skin, that no make-up colours their mouths, that there is no smudge of eyeshadow on their eyelids or slick of eyeliner in the corners of their eyes. A natural look is always preferred.

He looks at her. She is indifferent; she doesn't even blink.

Still, he finishes his sermon:

—Those who are careful in these matters will be worthy of honour and dignity, but those who are negligent will not escape censure and criticism.

You stare at him in astonishment; the girl doesn't even

look up, her clean eyes showing not a trace of make-up. On the contrary, she spreads her legs wider, much wider, sitting in an almost intolerable position.

ARE THEY VISIONS?

I write, now that I have escaped that siege of words cut short, now that I can give them timbre, density, their true register, height and colour.

I write and I say:

Today Juana de Soto y Guzmán —or is she Lugarda Aldana de Villarroel?— takes her vows.

The sermon is magnificent, given by Don Manuel de Escalante y Mendoza and later printed. Only thus will he liberate the words from the calamity that incapacitates them, their lack of corporeality (as Saint Augustine and Saint Bernard claimed). The only effective antidote against voices 'that swiftly flee', the priest explains, is the printing press with its moulds, the best way to persuade and delight the devout in repeated edification.

Now cloistered, Juana de Soto y Guzmán will take the name Sister Teresa Juana de Cristo.

Don Manuel de Escalante y Mendoza, Jesuit priest, specifies:

—Baptised Teresa,

confirmed Juana,

and de Cristo today, when she takes her religious vows.

He pauses and then resumes:

—The name Teresa means cleanliness, deriving as it does from 'tersa', which means clean and pure. Juana means grace, and today she is said to be of Christ because he is the Lord to whom she is betrothed and to whom she commits to being gracious, pure, clean, and exacting in all things.

Before the faithful gathered in the church, and before the nun crowned with flowers, the priest, bearing on his chest an enormous emblem depicting the Holy Child, goes on: —Let others celebrate the obedience of the sun, for I must celebrate that of this girl, Juana de Soto y Guzmán, this new moon with milk still at the edges of her lips, Juana, who, with a successful life ahead of her, leaves the world and commits to an obedience that is death, to a death that is obedience.

I pause, stop writing, I have tired myself out. I shall wait for a new moment of inspiration. Or would it be better to call it a vision?

SHE KEEPS TIME

On the record you're listening to, the trumpets sound the final note, bright and metallic. You are reminded again of the first cellist in that concert you liked so much, that day with him and the girl at Bellas Artes.

She is a foreign-looking cellist, Polish, perhaps. Actually, there are several women in the orchestra playing the cello, sitting in a row near the audience: The Slavic woman is one of them, her blonde hair cut short like a pageboy, her body long, her back well supported by the chair. She keeps time with her long, wide feet, tapping them firmly on the floor, lifting her toes as her heels remain in place.

Despite her masculine appearance, the cellist is graceful as she moves her hands on the instrument, handling the bow. She follows the rhythm with her head, her legs spread wide, her long skirt very full and asymmetrical, its fabric fluid, delicate.

Another of the cellists attracts your attention. She is plump, and her long skirt is of a less fine, less practical fabric; she spreads her legs to be able to play, but keeps her feet together, clad in high heels; she seems to be following the rules, the instructions:

'Women must close their legs when they sit.'

And spontaneously you turn around and look at the girl who has accompanied you to the concert. Today she is wearing neither the blue trousers nor the white shirt, and you know that if she had wanted to play the cello she would never have done it with her legs half-closed, as a mother superior in a convent would have wanted, as your lover would have wanted.

The girl is sitting unusually well, like a young lady, with her legs together, her back very straight, and her hands resting, softly, delicately, on her full, flowery skirt. Her nails are long and dirty.

A GOLD RING AS A SYMBOL

As I write, her name is now Sister Lugarda de la Encarnación.

Isn't there another nun with her, named Juana Teresa de Cristo?

One of them, I'm not sure which, says:

—You will be chosen and crowned with a divine crown in Paradise. You can consecrate yourself in the Holy Faith and wear a gold ring as a symbol of your excellence and incorruptibility. You are the most beautiful thing in the Holy Catholic Church and deserving of this precious reward. You are queen of heaven and of the earth, thanks to the fervent melody of contemplation.

And so, Teresa Juana hands Lugarda the scourges and she punishes herself. Blood spills softly, dripping down her back. Her breasts are erect. One nipple is reddened, its areola very rosy and rough, while the other breast is round, perfect, smooth-skinned, soft, with nothing interrupting its perfect sphere.

At that moment I interrupt my writing to say:

—Love that begins as lava ends up barren.

I am probably remembering that trip we took to Lanzarote and the eruption that devastated the island for six years, and which also left me consumed, arrested, eroded, like Sister Lugarda de la Encarnación's body after the flagellation, the hair shirts, the fasting.

RULES OF BEHAVIOUR

I tell you stories to distract you from thinking about him so much. I tell you the story of the young woman who played the cello and was sent by her parents to a convent.

The girl watches us in delight. She likes the story of the young woman, she likes that the young woman played the cello, she likes that in order to play it she had to adopt a position similar to the one that men adopt when they ride horses.

She is shocked, however, that the young woman had to stop playing: the mother superior at the convent where she was educated thought the position women had to adopt while playing the cello was obscene: sitting with their legs spread wide.

SHE IS GRACIOUS, PURE, EXACTING

——*What should I call her, when I write, her I mean? Sister Lugarda de la Encarnación or Sister Teresa Juana de Cristo?*

I am wearing a serious, dark blue dress that covers my arms, neck, and legs.

It doesn't matter, I think, immediately putting my fingers on the keyboard, it doesn't matter, it's enough that I'm writing, that I'm writing her. When I do, it's like I can see her and that's why I write, I write the following:

Juana de Soto y Guzmán is gracious, pure, and exacting. Her body is thin, very thin, and when she strips from the waist up before she flagellates herself, her breasts are notable for their enormous size.

They stand out, set there on her body, on a chest so narrow, bent by a delicate back, on a body so tender, a body that has seen so few dawns. And it is no great wonder, nor is it strange, nor prodigious, that this child, so newly fledged, should be so tender and green that there may as well be a trail of milk running from her lips to her mother's breasts.

Sister Lugarda de la Encarnación —or Sister Teresa Juana de Cristo?—

has large, asymmetrical breasts: one has an areola that is rough and pink, same as the nipple, although the latter is a more intense colour (almost scarlet). The other breast is round and soft as an apple. There is no break in its roundness. The breast is even, whole, with no areola to interrupt its smoothness. It is reminiscent of Eve's stomach before original sin, back before the beauty of our first parents included a belly button.

Do her enormous breasts not hide a sacred metaphor?

Does the Virgin not always appear nursing the Holy Child? Does she not show her breast in symbolic love when she intercedes with God on behalf of sinners? The same sinners who

Christ comforts and saves with the blood that flows from his side, blood that nourishes them like mother's milk, the sinners he redeemed with that precious liquid, the blood that flows from the open wound in his side.

Lugarda turns to Christ, to his flayed, wounded image, nailed to the Cross, and, imploringly, says these words to Him:

—Beloved, remember me now, sitting triumphant at the right hand of your Father, our Eternal Father. Keep me near you, inscribed on your hands and on your feet, lying on your sweet chest. Never forget me, Lord, never forget my soul, this soul that belongs to you and that you redeemed with your precious blood.

And just as the Virgin takes her breast delicately, Christ adopts an identical pose, offering his side, placing his middle and index fingers in the bleeding wound to show his injury, an injury from which redemptive blood flows, the blood of his breast, the blood with which he nurses his children on earth.

Would it be sacrilege if I were to compare those divine breasts with those of Sister Lugarda de la Encarnación?

Lugarda imitates the gesture in the image, using her index and middle finger to squeeze her left nipple while with the other hand she shows her Lord the other breast, that round, immaculate breast.

Would it be sacrilege to claim that the key difference, that one of her breasts has a mark on it and the other a total absence of marks, allows us to glimpse a heavenly sign, a sign that she is chosen?

That ritual, beautiful shape, gravely wounded, bleeding.

TROPICAL MUSIC

—Dance! he says, and you dance.

The music is tropical, salsas, rumbas, congas, guarachas. You stumble, following the rhythm reluctantly, and he gets impatient, grabbing your waist tightly until you pick up the rhythm again, matching the pace of the other couples dancing. It's some half-remembered New Year's Eve at your place, a flat overlooking the park entirely blanketed in snow. You are wearing barely any make up and an outfit that is cheap, nondescript, like everything else, the food, the music, the guests.

The girl is asleep in the bedroom and you worry that the music will wake her; you stumble again, paying less attention to the rhythm. He is increasingly impatient, scolding you, and you try distractedly to pick up the steps again; it's impossible. He slaps you in front of the guests. The blows resound, your cheeks burn, the music goes on, the dancers stop and stare. You hear the girl crying. You do not cry, nor do you respond to the blows.

The girl appears suddenly in the door of the living room. She is wearing red pyjamas.

YOU KNOW EXACTLY WHO HE IS

You obey, you know exactly what your master wants, you know exactly who he is, what he needs, what he does not, what he wants, what he does not.

—That's what turns you on so much, isn't it?

—I don't know why you ask, you reply, since you know perfectly well.

—Does he know?

—I don't know, but I think if he didn't he wouldn't act like that. He prefers to pretend he doesn't know, to act like he doesn't know.

An acrid taste in the mouth, like the smell of concentrated urea from the wall opposite. Saliva is thick, sticky, and contains an acid that protects your teeth from pain, made of clove extract.

—It tastes like poison, doesn't it? Or is it arsenic? No, hemlock.

—There's no need to exaggerate. You love melodrama.

A LONG BLACK SILK GOWN

It's still hot. The same kind of suffocating heat you felt when you went with him to that concert, the day a countertenor sang a Caccini ode in falsetto, an ode written for a castrato in the seventeenth century.

The basso continuo is played on the viola da gamba by a French woman wearing a long black silk gown, her legs spread as wide as they will go, her feet planted firmly on the floor.

The voice holds an intense, ambiguous note, the same note produced for you by that virile man, that perfect man with his broad, muscular body, and you hear that strange, high-pitched voice emerge from his visibly veined throat, a voice that perhaps resembles that of the castrato singer you heard in that concert (he sang Caccini's ode, many years ago, in Italy) or the man who sang the odes to Saint Cecilia.

You and I are listening to him right now.

SHE IS COLD

You and he have made up. You agree to go with him to the convent. You enter the cloisters. The girl plays near the orange trees in her blue trousers and white shirt.

You like the cloisters, the columns surrounding you, their capitals bearing monsters and demons, each figure different, asymmetrical. The infinite possibilities of evil?

You lean, pensive, completely motionless, against a column; above you, crowning your head, flies a little devil. You hold your breath. You are exhausted, you both are, practically turned to stone. A strange peace surrounds you. Your dry hair is pulled back very tight, austere; he looks like San Sebastián, looking up with that fine profile of his. What love reveals in you is sadness, yet despite it all, you start to feel happy.

The girl tires of playing and comes over; she is cold, she says. You both look at her, him in silence, you with a sigh, then you take her by the hand and start walking out of the cloisters.

He walks behind, following.

DISTINGUISHING FEATURES

I write her, the one who out in the world bore the name Lugarda Aldana de Villarroel —or Juana de Soto y Guzmán—

and then later, after taking her vows, Sister Lugarda de la Encarnación —or Teresa Juana de Cristo—

and she says:

—Because I am a foreign woman and a pilgrim in this land, I solemnly declare that I am not a daughter of man but

rather of God, and that I conceal myself in the appearance and figure of a woman. I declare before God that I am neither my mother's nor my father's daughter, nor I am my brother's sister, nor my sister's sister, though they may claim it to be so, and if they claim it to be so they are lying, because I do not belong to them. And if they bring witnesses who point to me and find distinguishing features on my body, my skin and my flesh — moles, scars, birthmarks— I solemnly swear again that I am not who they say I am.

She pauses and then goes on, in an exalted tone.

—We are all orphans, we have neither father nor mother on earth, because our Father is in heaven and our Mother is a Virgin. We come from there, not from here, and so I swear again, before God, that we are not of this earth.

Frightened by Lugarda Aldana's will, her parents decided to respect it. Her father suffered as though she were his only daughter, but her mother —her earthly mother, or was it her sister?— held a terrible resentment in the depths of her soul. She quietly decided she would go with her to the convent, and when it was her turn, she would cloister herself too, to show her that she was blood of her blood and flesh of her flesh.

She decided that with her own hand she would carve other distinguishing features onto her body.

I am exhausted, after writing her.

TEMPERANCE

I know very well, which is why I am writing it here, I know that some convents maintain the custom, after the nuns have risen, after prayer, by way of spiritual nourishment, of taking a freshly laid hen's egg and passing it carefully over their eyes until its gentle warmth has entirely cooled.

At this moment, as I rest my fingertips on the keyboard, Teresa Juana is taking this precaution after her prolonged vigils, her agitations of the spirit, that sudden passage from great darkness to very intense light that tires and mars the beauty of her eyes considerably.

Those eyes that serve only to adore God, to look upon him devotedly, to see him bleeding and passionate on the Cross.

I finish writing, get up, head for the kitchen, take a recently laid egg and pass it over my eyes several times. I feel its rough texture caress my eyelids, can almost feel, almost smell the yolk's yellow consistency. I know that when I rest my fingers on the keyboard again, the visions will reappear, in their pure and luminous transparency, before my eyes. The egg is an antidote for disappearances.

YOUR READING MATERIAL

This morning I see you absorbed in reading, so absorbed that you don't even realise I'm reading what you're reading over your shoulder:

'Ladies who ride horses, and especially those who ride astride the horse, soon develop a particular gruffness of the voice and their face takes on a tanned colour that disfigures any lady. The bones of the lower part of her body tend to misalign and impede the functioning of their femininity, a subject on which I need not dwell, for obvious reasons. Moreover, riding overdevelops her muscles and produces a disproportionate increase in her waistline, transforming her body and making it, in short, unfeminine.'

—What are you reading? I ask, although I have already read it.

You startle, look up, answer:

—It's a Victorian exercise manual.

—You're thinking of the girl? I conclude. You know that that's the kind of thing she does; the kind of thing he doesn't like, the kind of thing that was forbidden to women, and of course, especially, to girls.

You nod and reply:

—Exactly, Lilith was expelled from Paradise because she wanted to ride Adam as though she were a man.

THE PLACES OF THE HEART

You know very well that sometimes your heart does not lie in your chest.

You know very well that sometimes it lies between your legs. You recognise this to be the case right now. You know that in moments like these you may as well be a dog.

You understand the terrible strength of your desire.

Your body and his are one, you cannot separate them.

Let those who have never felt like a stranger to themselves cast the first stone! The Holy Scripture says so, does it not?

FROM THE BALCONY YOU CAN SEE THE STREET

You look again and see them in the courtyard. The dogs are both lying on the ground, their fur rumpled together, one brown, the other much lighter. As usual, the male starts sniffing the female, licking her and then mounting her; he moves at length on top of her, the two of them locked together; he gets off her and then urinates against the wall. You watch, as usual, captivated.

From the balcony you can see the street and the man urinating on the wall opposite.

You remember that when your lover urinates inside you, you feel pleasure in the same unconscious, natural way that the female dog feels pleasure.

What's more, you would like him to stay inside you for longer, like the dogs.

Pierced by him, nailed to him, knotted to your guts.

SHE DESPAIRS

I know exactly why I say it.

That's why I write her, that's why I write:

A heart overcome by love belongs to itself no more.

Lugarda confesses her sins, confesses that she has sought the Lord with all her strength, with all her soul, with all her body and has not been able to find Him. She despairs.

In church, she listens to Father Manuel's sermon.

He seems to respond to what she is thinking with the words of Saint Augustine:

—I seek my God in every corporeal nature, terrestrial or celestial, and find Him not: I seek His Substance in my own soul, and I find it not, yet still I have thought on these things, and wishing to see the invisible things of my God, being understood by the things made. I have poured forth my soul above myself, and there remains no longer any being for me to attain to, save my God.

Lugarda trembles.
Don Manuel ends his sermon:
—Since we are carnal, it must be that our desire and our love shall have its beginning in the flesh.
O, the heart throbs, burns, bleeds!

IN THE FOETAL POSITION

When you sleep alone you do not take off all your underwear; if you are naked, contact with the sheets is enough to make a shiver run through you. You need something to protect you from direct contact with the bedclothes. If you are completely naked you will inevitably be turned on and end up lying on your back, knees up, rubbing your nipples with controlled fury, one forefinger on your clitoris, moving rhythmically, making sure your nipples are always erect, almost painfully so: to achieve this you must alternate hands, your left hand on one nipple and a right finger on your clitoris, or your right hand on your other nipple (you can stroke your areola, pinkish, rough) and your left hand between your legs. Sometimes it is better to take off the rings you wear on the finger you use to masturbate.

Of course, the ideal thing would be for him to masturbate you like that, he could even do it through your underwear, of course, why not? He could insert his forefinger into your vagina and make your desire rise, then take off your clothes to kiss you, as he often does, though he rarely kisses you on the mouth or sticks his tongue in with your tongue.

But you are alone, so it's better that you remain composed, keep your underwear on, sleep on your side in the foetal position, your legs drawn up, or rather bent, carefully bent so as not to hurt your spine.

When he is there, don't try and get comfortable in some other position, rather, put your nightie on or make him wear pyjamas so you can fall asleep in each other's arms without feeling any desire.

If he doesn't sleep in your bed, the girl – sometimes – joins you.

HER EYES REVEAL A DESIRE

The girl in the portrait intrigues you. For a while now you have been mentioning her regularly whenever we talk. You are intrigued by her slight smile, her thin, pink lips, her ambiguous gaze, her make-up free eyes (you would perhaps have put make-up on her, make-up defines the gaze). Her unpainted face distresses you, her un-lined eyes make you wonder what she would look like made-up (in eyeliner, eyeshadow, blusher, hair curled or cut short).

Those unmade-up eyes reveal a desire (much like that of the girl lying on the sofa with her legs spread, in her blue trousers and white top?)

THE BLACK VEIL

Fights are good for writing. I pick it up again, and by doing so I continue to see Juana, and then also the other one, Sister Lugarda de la Encarnación.

Once they have taken their vows and are in their cell, Sister Juana Teresa de Cristo and Sister Lugarda talk to Jesus, their husband, their beloved:

—*My beloved Lord, for you I abandoned my father and my mother, my brothers and sisters, for you I left the riches of the world…*

She wilts suddenly, her face covered with a black veil, a sign of her widowhood, that she is the wife of a dead husband. Then she recovers, reveals her face and goes on with her prayer:

—*Did you know, my beloved Lord, that even if I had a thousand worlds under my command I would leave them for you, for you, the life of my soul? I have neither father nor mother, you are my father, you are my mother and I desire no other.*

Another voice murmurs in chorus:

—*Are you not my father and mother and much more besides? The mother who bore me in her belly laboured through childbirth for barely a day and a night, while you, sweet, beloved Lord, agonised so lovingly for me and bore me within you your entire life! And when the moment came for you to birth me, your labours were so intense that your blessed sweat transformed into blood, emerging from your body as drops that nourished the earth.*

O, sweet Lord of mine, has there ever been a mother who suffered the pains of childbirth like you did? When the hour of your liberation sounded, the hard Cross was your bed, your nerves and veins were bursting! And it could have been no other way: in a single day you gave birth to the whole earth, illuminating it!

I put down my pen, leave Lugarda and Teresa Juana talking passionately to their Divine Husband. I remove my fingertips from the keyboard and see the nuns immobile, silent, kneeling as they pray.

A FULL, RED SKIRT

I know you know it by heart, I know you are sick of me saying it, but it's good for you to hear, it's good to remember that figure replaced by another, the young woman painted over when her husband ordered her to be erased from the portrait. And yet she is there, upright, smiling, with her rosy cheeks, her un-made-up eyes, her red riding skirt.

She has been rescued by the restorer, little by little, century by century, and her husband rides behind her in the same painting, in the original version, now restored, displayed in the museum, the painting you saw with your lover, who mounts you, down on all fours.

Perhaps the lovers of the young woman in the portrait mounted her in the same way. She has reappeared, riding like a woman, side-saddle on her horse, her long skirt covering her legs.

SHE IS QUIET A LONG TIME

Lugarda makes me uneasy. She either talks a lot or is quiet for long periods of time. I spy anxiously on her, and as soon as she utters the first phrase I write it down, word for word:

—*Jesus has a real body and a mystical body on this earth. We adore his real body through Holy Communion, the Eucharist, and we adore his mystical body through communion with the Church.*

The mystical state is ineffable, it escapes intelligence and sight.

DELICIOUS PAIN

When you are with him, your body often rises off the ground due to the perfect union between your two bodies, as if what is heavy has become light. It's not that your bodies have lost their gravity but that the union is so perfect that when you melt into him your bodies' gravity lifts off the floor.

You always wished you were dying of that disease, of that pleasure and that pain, that arrow piercing your insides, that delicious shame.

You always wished you were dying of that disease.

At other times, you can barely keep your balance. You are still on the floor on all fours, like a thing transported, barely wheezing. You let out a few moans, not too loud, because you can't take it anymore. It's always like a sigh, a unique pleasure, delicious pain, for he gives it to you so hard that your whole body aches, you can't even move your hands or feet.

You always wished you were dying of that disease.

THE BED OF THISTLES

In all the Holy Scriptures, everyone knows, love burns keenly. I recall:
'The wife in the Song of Solomon called her husband to share a bed full of flowers, painted with roses and lilies, carnations and stocks.
The husband doesn't like such flowery, comfortable beds. The best bed, the one he likes the most, is a bed of thistles.'
And I repeat:
'Love burns more keenly that way.'

IT DAMAGES THE SPINE

And now he wants to make love in a different way. It's not that you don't know this position, you do know it, you know it well: if a woman is on her back on the bed she necessarily has to open her legs to receive the man. You don't understand it, you don't understand his whims, but you obey.

Hadn't he reassured you that the most natural position, the one that is least damaging to the spine, is the way dogs do it, the best way for your body to support the man's weight?

Hasn't he always told you that he hates women who spread their legs?

Didn't he censure women who rode horses like men?

Doesn't he scold the girl when he sees her lying on the sofa with her legs spread, dressed in her blue trousers and white shirt?

No, he doesn't really want you to spread your legs, he wants you to receive him. Once he is inside, he pushes your legs with his own so that you keep them closed, and you squeeze him like that, so it hurts more and you experience incomparable pleasure.

—You liked that, more than you've ever liked it before, didn't you?

YOU CATCH HIM LOOKING

You are on the bed. You feel his gaze on your back; he leans towards you, puts his finger between your labia and moves it, and you adjust to his rhythm. You catch him looking at your body and he makes you feel like your curves are perfect, your buttocks round and rosy like a cherub's, like that cherub you once saw together in the church, from behind, caught in winged movement, imperceptible, like your hips moving gently to the rhythm of his finger, deep inside you, until your labia are wet. He suddenly gets on top of you, you feel his penis clearly and then you turn over, he enters you and says:

—Put your finger between your labia!

And you do it immediately, and as you do, you graze his penis and can no longer contain yourself.

—Did you come?

You did. He could not. He comes more easily the way the dogs do it, but he is insatiable. He wants her, he wants the father, he wants the mother, he wants the girl, he wants the other man, the maiden, the other girl, the father and the mother, but mainly he wants it doggy style.

—Do you think he can?

—Yes, I answer. I think he wants to do it, can do it, with her, doggy style, and that she, the bitch, wants to do it, can do it, with him.

THE EYES OF HER BODY

I can see her clearly: she is in the garden, there are no white flowers any more, her wings have fallen off and she cannot fly. Lugarda looks at herself in an empty, shaded garden, surrounded by demons, yet she is lying motionless on her bed, eyes wide open, dazzled.

She does not understand what impetus drives her, she does not understand the magnitude of the work required by body and soul, she does not yet understand the effort required to recuperate her vision, to see herself again surrounded by white flowers.

How can she placate them, how can she placate the horde of wild demons spying on her, surrounding her, turning her bed into a torture rack?

In this state she cannot think even a single good thought. She seeks the darkness of rest, though it costs her dearly. The crowd of demons is so great that they are snatching at her both inside and out!

She sees them with the eyes of her soul more clearly than with the eyes of her body.

So she asks the Lord, as best she can, asks him to help her. She sings psalms, one phrase at a time:

—O exquisite Lord, your loving wife beseeches you.

—O you, comfort for the afflicted, be my refuge, deliver me from all evil.

—Let the demons not follow me, let them not tempt me, let them not blind me.

—Help me, save me, protect me.

—Be my refuge, sweet Jesus.

His help arrives in the form of words; she hears them clearly, but she can see him neither with the eyes of the body nor the eyes of the soul.

—But where is the danger

—in knowing that God loves you?

—in knowing that those who bare themselves entirely will find me?

—in knowing the gifts I offer those souls?

—the different tastes with which I endow them?

—the ways I push them and perfect them?

Lugarda listens with all her might. An absolute silence surrounds her. She prays again, begging with all her soul:

—Blessed Lord, let me see your body!

She hears the voice again:

—Because if you could see the features of my face they would reveal to you my body!

STEALTHILY

When I say it, by which I mean write it, someone in turn interrupts my vision to tell me, stealthily, very quietly, frightened and wicked, that the devils used to keep Lugarda stretched out on her bed as though it were a torture rack.

ENCOUNTERS

You are wearing a formal, low-cut, black trouser suit with high heels. He compliments you, saying: 'You look like a goddess.'

He looks up, asks the tall, handsome youth behind the bar for a drink. He gives him a peculiar, urgent look. You observe the reaction; the young man pauses for a moment, then returns the look. You confirm that some kind of understanding has been established between them, a slight smile playing around the edges of your lover's lips; in turn, the young man sketches the beginnings of an already lascivious smile.

The meeting has been sealed between the man and the boy. You are entirely uninvolved, your glass raised, a perfect statue frozen in astonishment.

A STRANGE WHITE EFFLORESCENCE

When you return, your house looks beautiful to you. It calms you. You look up and on the red brick ceiling, near the rafters, you notice a strange white efflorescence.

Salt residue, you think. Where could that have come from?

You examine it carefully, start finding it on other walls, textures that make the paint flake off and fill the space with bright crystals, bright, but also abject.

Calm does not exist, for the house, as ever, reflects you.

MEN RIDE ASTRIDE THEIR HORSES

The girl is still there, still nine years old, lying on the sofa with her legs spread in her blue trousers and white top. Her eyes are closed. She does not seem to be listening.

Then you mention the painting, the painting you saw with him in that museum, the painting that so interested you and that repeatedly comes up in conversation.

—I don't understand, I say, this seems like a lot of fuss over an old painting.

—I'm tired of explaining it to you, you respond, it's because of the horse, or rather, it's because of the girl's position in the portrait. She's riding side-saddle, like a woman. Men ride astride their horses, spreading their legs, letting them hang over the horse's flanks.

—And why would that be important?

—Don't you know how Europa rode the bull? She was sitting not like a man riding a horse but sideways on its back, with both feet secured on the right-hand side, clutching one of the beast's horns in her left hand so she didn't fall.

In that encounter, you marvel at having found someone who, brushstroke after brushstroke, time after time, without fail, finishes the painting of your ghost.

DID YOU HEAR HER?

Sometimes, after making love, I try to hear her voice, and when I do, I write it down immediately.

I start like this, saying to myself:

—Did you hear her?

Then I add:

—How could I not hear her? Her voice resounds in my ears. It is the word of God.

—Yes, I repeat, the word of God, but of that hidden God, the God who has chosen her voice, the voice of she who spoke or said she spoke to him.

I know, I know that her word cancels out those of the other women, the words of her sisters, or rather, the women she calls her sisters, Sister Lugarda de la Encarnación and Sister Juana Teresa de Cristo.

—Can't you hear her? I ask myself again, and to prove I can hear her I write:

'…and whoever was in this prison, let it be understood she has lost her voice, both active and passive, and her place: and she shall be deprived of every legitimate act and every trade. And even if she is released from prison, she shall not therefore be restored to her former things, and even if she is restored to

her place, she shall not therefore be given a voice once again in the chapter, and even if she is given an active voice, she shall not therefore be given a passive voice, unless, as expressly stated, it is granted to her.

If she has fallen into the sin of sensuality, even if she should descend from her position asking for mercy and pardon, she shall in no way be received...'

EXEMPLARY BEHAVIOUR

As I write, Lugarda receives communion, and as she receives communion she reflects, meditates, reasons, hopes to save herself by complying fervently with the sacraments, especially this one, the Eucharist. She knows that the sacrament brings her closer to God. She knows that, thanks to the sacrament, she becomes flesh of his flesh, blood of his blood. She understands that Christ transforms his body and blood into the sacrament, and she repeats that it is his body, although sometimes she also calls it bread. She calls it bread because it sustains life, she calls it flesh and blood because it is the unity of his substance. Lugarda knows, or believes she knows, that at the same time he wants his body to signify the humanity he suffered on the Cross. Lugarda, the nun, Christ's beloved spouse, thinks:

—Even if we eat his flesh and drink his blood, we will not cure our corrupt, sickly nature unless we get closer to Him. Only through exemplary behaviour, only by receiving the flesh and blood of the Lord with true purity will we cure the disease.

Meanwhile, Teresa Juana is dying of grief, hunger and thirst, of hunger for his flesh, thirst for his blood.

THE PEOPLE'S ABODE

Exhausted, I write Sister Lugarda's exhaustion.

Lugarda is a Germanic name that comes from the root luit, *community, people, combined with the root* gard, *abode.*

Lugarda means the people's abode.

HER TROUSERS ARE BLUE

You have left your room, early in the morning. You are talking to the girl, lying on her favourite sofa, dressed as always in her blue trousers and white shirt.

She says:

—To receive a man, women must spread their legs.

You look at her in astonishment and ask:

—Where did you hear that?

The girl looks at you quietly.

She breaks the silence by adding:

—Women who play the viola da gamba or the cello, or those who ride horses as if they were men, have to do the same: spread their legs.

You realise that she has been following all your conversations, that she is repeating them word for word. You are frightened by your own indiscretion, your carelessness. You promise to be more discreet from now on. That's what you told me that night. You don't dare tell him.

A FAINT SMELL OF MANURE

It has been a long journey; you are in the sacred city. The high altitude worries you a little. You have just arrived, seen the mountains, the snowy summits, the towering peaks.

In the city you bought slippers made from soft leather with a faint smell of manure. It is cold and the room is tiny. You promise not to make love. It is the first night and your hearts might give out.

You undress, both leaving your slippers on and your gold chains around your necks. You lie down next to him. He does not move, but you stroke him with the tips of your fingers all over his body. You are turned on, you masturbate him, climb on top of him.

He kisses you on the mouth, you put your tongue between his teeth and when you get carried away and start rushing he stops you, pulls back, shows you his intense desire and asks you to take your time to enjoy it. You slow down, taking refuge in the memory of past pleasure and in the interrupted intensity of the present.

—Do you understand? he asks.

—I understand, you answer. I have understood how to excite each other in ways that make love grow tenderly and often as the flames build. I can still feel its delicious effects today, the effects of that burning love at altitude, the drop of blood on my tongue and the pale pink of your lips.

You love how cliché these encounters are.

THE SIN OF PRIDE

—Tell me, is it true that when you ride like a man you are committing the sin of pride?

You say, yes, it's true, you have committed the sin of pride.

—Do you remember Lilith?

—Yes, you reply, I remember her. Lilith was exiled from Paradise, precisely for wanting to ride Adam as though she were a man, long before Eve arrived in those celestial lands, long before I would have fallen back into that sin, the sin of a rider who rides like a man, who rides not a horse but her man, and what's worse, astride him, a vulgar Europa mounted on the Bull.

After saying it, a lustful look comes over your face.

—Do you enjoy making love like that? I ask.

—You know I do, you say, so why do you ask?

THE PATH FROM THE MOUTH TO THE HEART

I have been able to verify it and so now I am writing it. It has never been necessary for Lugarda to chew food to keep her body alive. It is enough for her to receive the host, to crush it between her teeth. To feel it travel along that path from the mouth to the heart and for it to linger on her palate.

If she hurries to swallow, a voice stops her: —Why, do you wish to do away with me so soon? At other times Teresa Juana feels as though soft hands or gentle waves were moving inside her mouth in loving combat.

And she usually divides the host between her teeth, splitting it into three fragments, one kept fixed to her palate, the other in her throat, and the third on its way to her chest, next to her heart. She feels as though she were being stroked by delightful hands or fanned by the beating of wings in a loving battle.

Teresa Juana looks at the Blessed Sacrament in her chest. Then she sees him as a pretty boy and, as she goes to receive him in her heart, as a beautiful girl. There, in the centre of her chest, they embrace, crowned with white roses.

STRANGE APPARITIONS

You are walking with him, him leading you by the hand as though you were a little girl. The girl follows behind, dressed as usual in her blue trousers and the same white shirt. Sometimes she follows slowly, at other times she hurries and tries to join you.

She puts on a spurt and manages to catch up, to walk next to you, in line; she reaches out her hand to yours – the one that's free – and strokes you with her nail, just very slightly, then slides her right hand into your left one so you form a threesome.

You have arrived. The room is large, the light from above illuminating the statues with a delicate glow. He shows you the one he especially likes, an ancient estofado depicting Saint Francis. There is something unusual about it, you think. You are used to this saint being dressed in a coarse tunic tied with a rope. These clothes are sumptuous, decorated with gold leaf and exquisite brocade trimmings worked over with heavy, dark brushstrokes to form strange flowers. A rough cord is cinched around his waist and the fabric on his chest is torn, allowing us to glimpse, elegant and symmetrical, the wound in his side, the bone showing through the flesh, the blood ruining the elegance of the attire and undermining its formality. To emphasise this, the saint's bare feet are resting on skulls.

You concentrate, trying to find the exact words to explain what you are feeling, the bitterness, the violence inflicted on you by the interrupted perfection of this statue. Just as you are about to utter the first word, the girl squeezes your hand and angrily sinks the sharp nail of her ring finger into your palm.

—What are you doing? you shout at her. That hurts!

—If it didn't hurt, I wouldn't do it, she murmurs.

You look at her, see her faint, triumphant smile, and push her, hard, you hit her angrily, raising your arm, a drop of blood trickling down your hand. Before you can stop her, she grabs it and licks delightedly at the little wound.

Your lover remains unscathed, still gazing enthralled at the saint. Around you, apparently absorbed, people are looking at the other statues and paintings.

SCRATCHES

I tell you a story, the one about a woman in the habit of leaving marks on her lover's skin, scratching his member with her (red-painted) nail, the same finger she sometimes uses to masturbate.

That very woman, at the exact same time you and he are making love, is listening to one of Bach's sonatas for harpsichord. She confirms, in that moment, something she has always thought: that the sound produced by the harpsichord player's fingers on the keyboard is equivalent to a scratch on the soul.

THE SOUL IS INEBRIATED

As I write, she—Sister Lugarda de la Encarnación— explains:
—From his blood Jesus created a drink and from his flesh he created nourishment for those who wished to be redeemed. There is no better way to satiate oneself, there is nothing like it…

An echo answers her. It is Teresa Juana:
—Hunger and thirst can only be assuaged with his body and his blood.

—Even if you possessed the whole world, you would be unsatisfied, desiring more, much more, more, much more. The world does not satiate, it does not calm, it is not enough. Nothing encompasses us in its entirety. Only blood satisfies, because blood is part of the divine…

—Eight days after he was born, Jesus spilled a little of his blood during circumcision, which must have cost us dearly, his blood starting to spill so early on, blood that was not enough to save humanity.

—It was the lance in his side that opened his heart and delivered us his blood.

They sing psalms together, passionate:
—And the soul is inebriated: devoured by thirst. The more the soul drinks, the more it desires to drink: the more it carries the Cross, the more it desires to carry it. The blood of the Lord is like the milk with which mothers nourish their sweet children. And pain is the soul's consolation, tears shed in memory of his blood are its drink and sighs its nourishment. And the heart bleeds, throbs, and burns.

ONE NOTE AT A TIME

You are naked, lying face down. Two girls are massaging you gently, systematically, conscientiously. They start with the legs, the insides of the thighs; first, they work with their hands, their touch light, almost non-existent, then with a vibrating device to remove the fat; little by little, as you are lulled to sleep, their soft voices reach you, snatched phrases, a delicate, suggestive murmur. Each girl takes one side of your body. One is called Teresa, of that you are sure; you do not know what the other is called.

Their hands move lightly over your back; it is a curious sensation, as though those young, wise hands were discovering certain parts of your body in a new way; a totally new way of feeling your body, which is used to him discovering it for you, an intense body, a body synthesised by pleasure, orbited around its centre, when he mounts you on all fours on the floor.

They take control of your muscles and revive them, as though pushing the flesh against the current, even though they have found its true course; you recognise your geography through their hands: the muscles of your neck, your slim waist widening into your hips. You calculate the weight of each of your vertebrae, the width of each of your toes, their pressure points, their sensitivity, the thickness of your toenails, and they stroke the soles of your feet with a strange electronic device, smooth, but with hidden needles that make you grimace. While the voices whisper, immersed in a daily routine alien to yours, they work on your body as though it were sponge-like, malleable, as though one by one they could reconstruct or create your muscles, your tendons, section by section of that vast expanse that now belongs entirely to you but which you leave in their hands. You also feel – strange thing – the weave of your blood, a perfectly articulated tangle of veins and arteries: you feel how they communicate proudly under your skin, a river flowing or a subterranean orthography that becomes visible thanks to its taut, swollen architecture. Health and beauty are not only carnal, they are sanguine, too. You think about the woman, that woman who seeks bodily destruction while here you are fine-tuning your hips, looking after your muscles. That woman whose veins shatter and burst, allowing blood to run over her flesh, leaving marks, bloody stripes, a different bodily weave.

Or again you remember, with a shiver, the weight of your lover as he mounts you, you remember his caresses, his slaps, the feel of him inside you. You emerge from that reverie, returning to where you are, a place where you are trying to mould your body. You realise once again that you do not exist for them, that your material existence has not the slightest importance there. The girls are working on your body, you are merely – I repeat – raw material to be moulded and reconstructed. For the first time, your body exists by itself – the girls' hands reveal it to you – it exists in a dimension other than that of love. It is suddenly whole, a body free of desire.

The fingers run over you, bringing to mind the delicate sound of fingers on a piano, Mozart's crystalline sonatas, the pianist building the melody one precise, clear note at a time, you can hear it, you feel the pauses like the pianist feels them in his fingertips, the pauses before a high, uneven sound, the note at a greater distance, as though the fingers might suddenly take a false step, to fall into the abyss: the note is reached after the patient accumulation of several clear sounds, one after another, perfectly separated from each other. Those notes resound in the soul.

In love, fingers play differently: the body is like a harpsichord keyboard, fingers hammering, wounding, snatching, even, because it's played with the very tips of the fingers, the nails, plucking, scraping.

FINGERS AND MARKS

A woman is in the habit of leaving marks on her lover's skin, grazing his member with her (red-painted) nail, the same finger she masturbates with.

That very woman, at the exact same time that you and he are making love, is listening to one of Bach's harpsichord sonatas. She confirms, in that moment, something she has always thought: the sound produced by the harpsichord player's fingers on the keyboard is equivalent to a scratch on the soul.

The marks leave a trace, inscribe a rhythm, allow a possibility, a pause. They soothe the anxiety of waiting, the arrival of the ghosts.

CONTINUOUS MOVEMENT

Yesterday, you were at a concert with him; yesterday, recorder music was being performed.

You took the girl.

The recorder player is thin, agile, his body more suited to the circus than the world of music. His hands and mouth, on the other hand, are perfectly musical.

He plays a Vivaldi largo on his tiny, sweet recorder. The high-pitched sound is vulnerable and his silhouette resembles the figure of the god Pan, moving, contorting.

A pause; he places the recorder in a case, takes out a longer one – quite a lot longer – and begins another piece. The sound is coarse and deep; the piece modern. His body convulses, jumping on the spot, producing erratic, almost disagreeable sounds: you feel a long shudder. The music stops suddenly. The player returns the long recorder to its place, a practical, theatrical case.

The audience coughs, people shift in their seats.

The girl is sprawled in her chair, spine arched, legs spread. For once she has agreed to wear a quite full, longish dress in a fluid, silky fabric with pink flowers on a blue background and a border – smocking, they call it – between pleats, moulding her flat chest. She has done the belt up tightly in a wide bow at the back. She seems absent, her hand tightly laced through yours. She is on your left.

Just when the player is pulling out two other, more traditional-looking recorders, your lover takes you by the hand. You feel him run his nails over your palm and the caress makes you tremble.

The performer places the two recorders on his knees, inserts stoppers – 'to amplify the sound of an octave' – your friend the pianist explains; she is sitting one row in front of you. The music is wonderful, the recorder player achieves miracles with his hands and mouth, the sound is slightly discordant, but you like it. You don't know why, at this precise moment today, you remember yesterday's concert; you are at home listening to Purcell's church music, the odes to Saint Cecilia, sung by a countertenor whose voice imitates those of the castrati (was the memory triggered by the countertenor's strange voice? What is the association with the recorder player?)

It feels like you are looking at him right now, playing the recorders, playing with them on his knees, stoppering and unstoppering the ends in a continuous, successive movement. Today you look back on it, you relive the concert you went to yesterday with them, with him and the girl, while you listen to the music marked by trumpet solos and voices in different registers, with the tenor, the countertenor, the soprano, the bass, the countertenor again and the trumpets' sharp, high-pitched, continuous note. You remember it today, yes, yesterday's extraordinary concert; especially the player with his recorders, the juggling, circus-like performer, like the monkey on the organ grinder, the player who right now in your memory takes out a giant recorder and transforms from the light, graceful god Pan into Priapus, handling the instrument as though he were performing fellatio.

And the voice of the countertenor, in strange, appealing registers, stands out among the trumpets in Purcell's ode, and the obscene recorder player emits strange, delightful sounds, and now you know. You know why you remembered, you know that you connected him with that piece of pre-Hispanic pottery in the shape of a grotesque character who sucks on his own penis.

Meanwhile, as you sit in your seat at the concert yesterday, just as the association becomes clear in your mind, the girl takes your hand and digs her nails into your palm.

You are about to cry out, to slap her, but the gentle sound of the recorder stops you.

SHE BEHAVES BADLY

—Is it true, I ask you, that when you mount him as if he were a horse or you were a man, you are committing the sin of pride?

Although you do not answer, I know you are thinking about it, because when you mention the matter you bring up Lilith, adding that for that very reason, for wanting to ride Adam as if she were a man, God exiled her from Paradise, long before Eve, who always adopted the only position reserved for women in bed.

The girl has probably been spying on us for a while. She appears, smiles maliciously and puts a finger in her mouth: she starts sucking it like a baby.

We have never managed to understand her, which is why you are looking at her in astonishment.

THE WHITE ROSES

I have seen how Lugarda cares for, caresses, fixes a disjointed Christ who in the Holy Sepulchre appears gravely wounded, and as she caresses him, crowning him with white roses, she says:

—My God, take these roses in place of your thorns, for I want to bury them in my heart.

She offers this flattery with such burning love that the Divine Figure is moved and answers her with his Divine mouth:

—Daughter, you are my flower and my gift, and like a white lily I wear you in my crown.

Lugarda despairs when she loses him, when his voice ceases.

And so every day she begins the search again: she looks for the flowers, the images, the thorns. It is the insatiable desire to find an answer to a pain, the pain born from the loss of the body, of that divine, sacred, beloved, everyday body, that body that evades her, that body that appears and disappears relentlessly, that body that never remains, a bleeding body, sometimes mute, a martyred body that sometimes cries out, but always a loving body, a space where the most terrible obsessions, the greatest pains and the biggest risks play out.

SIMPLE WORDS

You always feel guilty, you are always thinking about it, even when you're enjoying yourself, in even the best moments you're thinking about your guilt, that guilt that could perhaps be attenuated if you could explain, in simple, precise words, what made you do it.

You would like to speak to the girl and explain it to her, make her see that things couldn't have been any other way. Because it's not that you can't keep your mouth shut, but rather that you cannot open it to say the thing that would calm her rage and your shame.

You know full well, though – you can feel it – that in the precise moment you let him mount you, the guilt remains but your pleasure increases.

HE COMMISERATES
WITH HER SORROW

*L*ately, I've been writing little; when I do, she is crying, like me, crying night and day, and in her prayers she begs the Lord to lead her not into temptation: she hides her entire body from his eyes and touch, as far as human necessity will allow.

Finally, the sweet Son of Mary commiserates with her sorrow:

—My daughter, seeing as you have desired me with all your strength, with such determination, I wish to alleviate your suffering and therefore grant you the grace of seeing me.

And then Christ appears to her, naked, almost a child.

Dress me, Lugarda, he asks her, dress me, cover me as they cover my body in the church on the day of the Passion.

Lugarda, overcome, is fearful before her Divine Lover's nakedness, fearful because she does not know whether this changing vision (he is now a mature man) comes from God or from the Devil.

Immediately she hears the words of her confessor, Don Manuel, resounding in her head as he preached them. She remembers them clearly, can recite them by heart:

'The Blessed Virgin never saw nor touched her Son naked, she always saw him clothed in a dense and impenetrable light.'

Why then does the Lord allow himself these licences with her?

When he appears naked again, Lugarda rebukes him:

—O, sweet Jesus, even if it means you do not return, even if you distance yourself from me, even if I lose you forever, if you do not return honestly clothed and respectfully offering your love, I will not receive you again.

To stop him, to reassure herself that this was not a vision of the devil, she begins to pray aloud. Juana responds to her words:

—You…

—*Afflicted*....
—*Sorrowful*...
—*O! Sorrowful mothers*...
—*Virginal lilies*...
—*Handmaids of the Lord*...
—*Repeat with me*...
—*And with the Angel*...
—*Hail Mary, conceived without sin*...

They fall silent. Lugarda waits, scared he will not return.

And yet he does return, and, stunned, she watches him arrive, stern but gentle, scornful but loving, sometimes even pretending to absent himself.

And so she is tormented, both desiring and detesting the visions, flagellating herself furiously, wearing a cilice against her skin, wounding her body but caring meticulously for her hands so they remain virginal, like white doves, the greatest offering for her redeemer, and, entranced by love, she strokes him, the crucified, the blood-stained.

ON THE EDGE OF THE BED

You wish you had her determination, but you do not, because often (you have plenty of experience) your need is so extreme that it afflicts your soul, and that affliction reaches the point of becoming bodily.

The affliction of the body is terrible; your resolve wavers and you call him again. Since he suffers from the same pain, your lover returns. The astonishment you feel when you see him is so great that your bodily indisposition only increases.

He does not wait, but throws himself on you so violently that the pain and pleasure make you faint; the marvel begins and your body adopts the most incomprehensible positions, you lengthen, shrink, twist, and the strength of his embraces returns and you rise and fall over and over, contorting with a wild and painful desire, and your body and his are now a single body, extended, multifaceted.

You are exhausted. He sleeps beside you, but when you want to start things up again you get up and go to the edge of the bed and run your tongue over the soles of his feet, slowly, not forgetting the toes.

It is foolish to unleash the body's potential and then think that it could remain still.

LOVE OF MY LIFE!

Sister Lugarda de la Encarnación had a vision as I was writing this.

She saw Christ, bare-chested, and that image was consolation to her, because she was seeing Jesus as though he were a real mother, a mother in one of her tenderest moments, while nursing her children

(blood spills from the wound in his side),
and suddenly she saw him as a lover
(he looks at her with burning love),
Lugarda confesses,
or was it Sister Teresa Juana de Cristo?
Is it she who exclaims...?
—O, beloved God, o! Love of my life, I can no longer see you, but I know you were here!

YOU ARE ASTONISHED

Every time you look at the girl, her face astonishes you. It is an even colour, neither white nor nut coloured. It is, of this you are certain, a lovely colour, and you notice that her skin is increasingly perfect and smooth. Her eyes shine with a peculiar light, combining the most perfect innocence with a hint of lust. The girl's feet are bare and emit that same warmth, an outpouring contained in her long toes: when they curl up in their natural way they immediately provoke desire. The folds of her body are delicate, adorable.

Her nails have grown too long and are very dirty. When she hears him come in, she runs to the door, shows him her bare feet and hands him the clippers she has ready in her right hand.

HIS HEAD IS LEANING

When I come, when I am overcome by love, when I reach ecstasy, I want to go back to writing Lugarda de la Encarnación. When I start writing, at the moment I place my fingertips on the keyboard, she is asleep.

Near her cell, in the oratory, there is a statue. It is the size of a human body, and none of its limbs has the slightest flaw in its symmetry or proportion. The man's head is leaning on his left shoulder and his countenance is so pitiful that there is no one, no matter how distracted, no matter how brief their glance, who, on seeing him, will not find their heart melting in tears of compassion.

Juana wakes up and opens her eyes. She has received some kind of call. She gets up from her bed and goes to the oratory to where something —Someone?— is directing her footsteps. She finds the sacred image scratched and wounded. She cries, stroking it. In a frenzy, she starts torturing herself, scratching and wounding her own body until it is identical to the statue's. Their blood is the same colour, crimson, fresh, bright.

That is when I stop writing.

TENSE HANDS

He is on top of you. I can only see his back, a fragment of darkness where your face must be, and your tense hands, one stroking his skin and the other, the right hand, sinking sharply into his flesh one nail at a time.

The bed creaks and your nails dig deeper into his skin. Then everything is calm.

You sigh and ask:

—Did you come?

He does not respond. He is exhausted.

Your claws have left marks on his skin.

YOU RAISE YOUR ARMS

You are lying on your back on the bed, your pubis dark brown and curly. Your arms are raised, your underarm the same colour as your pubic hair, also curly. He looks at you, leans over and kisses your underarm one after the other. Then he finds your mouth and sticks his tongue between your teeth. You bite it; this turns him on enormously, as always, and, as always, he immediately asks you to masturbate, knowing it excites you, and you obey, you stick your finger between your labia; he straightens, enters you, you bend your legs and knot them around his back, you feel the blow against your cervix and speed up the rhythm.

You raise your arms, put your hands on his flesh, supporting yourself there, digging the nails of your right hand into his back – his olive skin – and feel the blood run in little droplets down your fingertips.

Later, you lick it.

Reddish striations leave a reminder of the passage of your nails down his back.

SHE STRIPS TO THE WAIST

It's been a long time since I had the strength, the strength needed to write her, that strength that drives me to visit her, that strength that makes me duplicate them. They are two now: one Lugarda, the other Juana.

And as soon as I decide to write, Lugarda says to Juana:

—Juana, give thanks to God that he raised you to belong to him. Follow his voices.

And Juana listens to the voices.

And the voices said that she should replace her delicate Dutch linen with a coarse tunic, replace her sheets with ones whose wrinkles would hurt her entire body, that she should sleep on nothing but two boards with nothing to support her head, that she should have no bedclothes except a thin blanket to cover her naked body; that on her arms, her waist, her thighs she should tie a belt made from horsehair and steel chains; that she should put little stones and sometimes sharp nails in her shoes, and when Lugarda falters, Juana should take up her discipline to help her, and, after asking her to strip to the waist, should rain down lashes on her back and then run sharp nails over the fresh wounds.

And Juana does it with such perfection that the marks on Lugarda's body remain intact and are not allowed to heal.

Since penance offers rest and relief from her sorrows, when she carries it out she believes she is in heaven among the choirs of angels. Does she perhaps identify with Saint Teresa? Did the angel not approach Teresa on the day of Ecstasy? Did Jesus not pierce her heart with an enormous spear? Is that not the symbol of their sacred marriage vows?

CAPTIVATED

I surprise the two of you in bed. I like watching you, the two of you, reflected in the mirror, studying the different positions you adopt when you make love. I like describing them as though they were images on picture cards.

Right now your bodies are forming a strange figure. It is impossible really to tell which body is mounting the other: it looks like the heads are separated from the torsos because of the distorted poses your desire has forced you into. One head – is it his? – seems to have been chopped off, and yet it is alive, you can tell by the intense pleasure in its eyes, eyes unfocused in awe, and by the half-open, exhausted mouth. Of you, I can barely see your hair and a fragment of your mouth and cheek, the rest is shadow.

And now I see your legs: they are drawn up and spread wide, balancing precariously, and your arms – yours or his? – are supported on the floor like a gymnast's.

As I watch, it looks like your body has grown several limbs, allowing you to catch him and keep him in that severed, motionless pose, and make his head, thanks to this definitive framing that intertwines your bodies, sketch confidently a picture in which life and death exist on a continuum.

This is how you suffer – along with him – a torment even more delicious than that produced by a body with only two legs. In that encounter, you marvel at having found someone who, brushstroke after brushstroke, time after time, without fail, finishes the painting of your ghost.

SUBMITTED TO A DESIRE

You know it's true what I'm saying, the girl not only rides horses like a man, she also has an imaginary viola da gamba between her legs.

Then you look at her.

The girl smiles as she bares her feet, revealing long, dirty toenails.

She takes the clippers and says:

—It's been ages since I cut my nails.

At that moment he comes in and stares at her, rapt.

Sometimes, other people too seem subject to a desire, even if it's only an impulse.

THE GAUNT BODY

I say (I write):
—I don't know if it's true what I say, because, though I've heard it, I'm not sure I remember rightly.

If only I could remember those words, perhaps they would help Lugarda de la Encarnación (when I write her) to further ignite that love she feels for Christ and for his gaunt, bloodstained, crucified body.

FOOD IS SEASONED

*I*n Lugarda's convent, I know full well, for I have seen it, that food is seasoned with aloe juice, ash, and wormwood.

Since the house was old and the cells were teeming with foul bedbugs, Teresa Juana ordered her sisters, with more than lukewarm spirit, to collect as many as they could and bring them to her cell. Each came with a handful or little tube of bloodsuckers and, as if they were delicate sweets or some tasty snack, began to eat them, following Lugarda in offering the Lord the repugnance of such a revolting feast.

If you are subject to self-love, do not read this!

If you are a slave to taste and to your stomach, do not read this!

SPIRITUAL EXERCISES

You lie half-naked on the bed, waiting for him. You like this, you love that he comes and helps you undress, that he caresses your breasts, that he starts kissing you little by little, every part of your body, millimetre by millimetre, you love that he puts his hands inside the underwear you are still wearing and strokes you between your legs. You like that he then starts taking off that last piece of clothing, and that when you are completely naked he asks you to lie on your front, that he contemplates you for a moment, strokes you, puts a finger between your labia, and you wait delightedly, impatiently, for him to throw himself on you, to feel his erect member on your body, for him to turn you over, wanting violently for him to enter you, feeling him stand, mount you, penetrate you, and because your legs are pressed tight together it both hurts and turns you on enormously, until there is no doubt that he is inside you and you, so far gone, inside him.

THE VOICES OF THE NUNNERY

Whenever I return to writing, I see Sister Lugarda de la Encarnación exhausted, motionless on the bed, embracing a crucifix, much like the other women in their abandonment, the nuns who dissolved themselves for love of God; their desire is so great that they wilt and are for long periods of time immobile, incapable of making the smallest movement or of getting out of bed (so great is their passion and so deep their contemplation); the sisters do not suffer any illness; their souls have reached a state of dissolution through love of Christ; with Him their spirit is comforted and their body wanes, their soul dissolves through the love of God and their cheeks are drawn; they can digest only divine nourishment, for earthly food makes them nauseous; tears have left tracks on their faces; one sister, in a state of intoxication, can remain still and silent for days at a time, without hearing even the voices of the nunnery or the din of the outside world; many, when they receive communion, taste sweet milk and honey: the sweetness of the heart of Jesus has reached their spirit; when they receive the bread of the Lord their soul is soothed and a great consolation reaches their mouths, a taste sweeter than mother's milk; their desire is soothed when they have the Blessed

Sacrament between their teeth, and they can regain their calm: they regain it when they digest the sweetness of that heavenly nourishment, when they dissolve his body between their teeth; they are exhausted, white as wax, illuminated.

They do not digest, they do not urinate, they do not bleed.

Lugarda embraces the image after taking communion. The image writhes! Everything dissolves!

And just as when the sun comes out from behind a cloud, the great face of Christ our Lord appears, deeply afflicted, his hand on his right cheek and a horrible helmet of thorns on his head, his face completely covered in blood. And then suddenly he grows and swells until everything seems to be at boiling point.

His face is so anguished that his swollen lips part until you can see the white of his teeth; blood begins to drip from the right nostril, as bright and fresh as though from a fresh, healthy body. His face is livid, sullied; it looks as though blood is oozing all over his skin; his complexion is very smooth and shiny, his beard short and parted in two, his whole face a tableau of pain.

In short, her vision was so intense, her passion so sacred, that she cannot put it into words. And so Lugarda, gripping the cross tightly between her hands, blacks out and falls down in a faint.

THE BEAUTY OF HER EYES

I know full well, and I repeat it by writing it down, I know that some convents have the custom, after the nuns have risen, after prayer, by way of spiritual nourishment, of taking a freshly laid hen's egg and passing it carefully over their eyes until its gentle warmth has entirely cooled.

As I write, Teresa Juana is taking this precaution, after her prolonged vigils, the agitations of her spirit, the sudden passage from great darkness to very bright light that tires and mars the beauty of her eyes considerably.

Those eyes that serve only to adore God, to look upon him devotedly, to see him bleeding and passionate on the Cross.

THE AREOLA IS PINK

You are about to go to bed. Your nightshirt is nun-like, covering your legs right down to your ankles, and you are wearing black velvet slippers.

Your arms are completely covered by the sleeves, but your chest can be seen through a fine lace. Your breasts emerge, the rough pink areolae standing out amid arabesque patterns. The nipples are red, poking defiantly through the holes in the fabric.

You wait for him, but this time patiently. When he arrives, he lies down and runs his tongue over the lace. He sucks your nipples leisurely, playing with them as though he were a child, and you stroke him as though you were his mother. He continues sucking, leisurely, occasionally biting you.

IN DISTRESS

I continue the thread of my tale. Right now, Lugarda is confessing her sins, confessing that she has sought the Lord with all her soul, with all her strength, with her entire body, and with her heart.

Don Manuel listens and answers by citing Saint Augustine:

—I seek my God in every corporeal nature, terrestrial or celestial, and find Him not: I seek His Substance in my own soul, and I find it not, yet still I have thought on these things, and wishing to see the invisible things of my God, being understood by the things made. I have poured forth my soul above myself, and there remains no longer any being for me to attain to, save my God.

Don Manuel ends with the saint's words:

—Since we are carnal, it must be that our desire and our love shall have its beginning in the flesh.

Lugarda sighs; she has lost his image, that is why she is in distress.

The words of her confessor can calm neither her anguish nor her grief. She would like for the image, the one of the holy crucified Lord, to remain forever by her side, like the body of a lover. She would like to embrace it with her earthly arms, press it to her breast and feel the bleeding presence of his gaunt body upon her.

She pulls herself, finally, out of her state of distress, and exclaims:

—He who seeks not Christ's Cross seeks not the glory of Christ. He is my all, my wisdom; I know him, I make him exist in his true state. How delicately he wins my heart! My heart bleeds, throbs, burns.

CUPID OR ARCHANGEL?

Your breasts are small, set apart; the areola is very rough, the nipples bright red (some women have black or purple nipples, or even brown). He likes to look leisurely at you, lying on the bed, naked, in a garnet necklace and a brooch in the shape of an angel – cupid or an archangel, winged, with a column at its base supporting an apocalyptic moon on which the virginal feet are poised – a figure with a bevelled mirror in his hands.

A hybrid between Cranach, Titian and Echave Orio? And there are, of course, rings on your fingers, rings that, like your nails, leave marks on the body: tattoos or scratches.

I TAKE OFF MY SHOES

It is hot. I unbutton the neck of my dark grey dress bearing classic beige and white motifs. I take off my shoes, rest my feet on the floor, write:

I've been told, and so I am consigning it to writing, that during Teresa Juana's illness Lugarda tended to her with holy devotion, on her knees, watching her every movement.

She suffered terrible pains in her body as well as neglect, emptiness, and anguish in her soul.

To soothe her, Lugarda fed her with her own hands, and with her own hands removed the chamber pot from the cell.

The two sisters are each other's shadows.

A WALL

Crossing the road, you stop.

You have seen them: you see the dogs mating.

You have seen her too: about to give birth, the female dog drags her innumerable heavy teats across the ground.

Against the wall opposite, a row of men.

That's where the dogs urinate.

CARELESSNESS

You think, or so you told me, that it turned him on enormously one day when, in a moment of carelessness, you left the door ajar and he saw you urinating, standing up, leaning forwards slightly.

When you came out, he said:

—I want to urinate inside you.

And contrary to what you expected, you enjoyed it very much.

WOOL AGAINST SILK

You lie on the bed, naked, your eyes closed, legs spread. You hear him come in, hear him open the door, feel him approach, feel his gaze on your body. He opens his legs and climbs on top of you, as though riding a horse, forcing your own legs to close.

He is fully clothed and the fabric of his suit scratches your skin, its wool against the silk of the tights you still have on.

He bites your left breast and the sharp pain is soothed when he runs his tongue over your areola. You can differentiate the two textures, the roughness of the breast and the fibres of his tongue.

—Masturbate! he orders.

Obedient, you insert your forefinger into your vulva and move it at your own pace.

The same wetness on your nipple and in your vagina.

—Did you come? you ask him.

He has fallen, exhausted, on top of you.

AN UNLIKELY POSITION

While you wait for him, lying on the bed, you like looking at picture cards. Right now it's a Japanese one. The naked characters are in an unlikely position, a favourite position for lovemaking. She has small breasts and delicate nipples, and her tangled pubic hair forms a halo around her vagina, whose open labia allow us to see the pinkish flesh. She is holding the man's enormous, black, well-defined, menacing penis; in contrast, their faces are serene. He has a small, pointed object in his hand.

They are about to start coupling, their inexpressive faces crowned with the same implacable hairstyle, held in place with long pins. Their strictly pulled-back hair shows not a single loose strand.

—Does it turn you on, looking at those?

TEARS AND SIGHS

I'm writing again. I'm writing of her torments: I know, I've read and have been told, that she was in the habit of praying as though on a cross, and since Lugarda was so ardent in her prayer, it's easy to see how her body suffered in so violent a position.

When she went down to the refectory, she would often bear an extremely heavy cross on her thin shoulders; at other times she would discipline her back with not inconsiderable force; at other times she would arrive on her hands and knees like a beast, dragging heavy stones that left her with indescribable injuries, and, as though all that were not enough, she still confessed her most minor thoughts through burning tears and in the most hyperbolic terms.

Teresa Juana followed in her footsteps.

Their perfect union and their penance tugged at the heartstrings of even their greatest enemies and imitators, obliging them to interrupt their meal and join the weeping and sobbing until it became a chorus. I have been assured that, thanks to the behaviour of those two women, many nuns improved their lives, forgetting about the world. Would that all could follow their example.

DISCORDANT VOICES

He seems to be watching you as you sit, excited, next to him in the theatre, where you've come to see to an opera. A performance of Strauss's Elektra.

The voices break; they are no longer singing but rather crying out on stage: you told me later that when you heard them they instantly reminded you of those wounded figures in church, the bloodstained Christs, fresh scabs, newly opened wounds. The voices are dissonant, discordant, and yet they harmonise, expressing their lament with admirable energy. She – the contralto – crawls, wild, howling like a dog.

You understand that God is in the details, in the intonation, in the scarlet colour of the curtains descending into the abyss; in the ruins of props, in the stage covered in the blinding colour of blood.

On hearing her laments, the contralto's laments, you are reminded of your own moans, excited moans in the moment of lovemaking, the moment of most extreme pleasure. In your memory, he has put his index finger in your mouth and your teeth produce a slightly viscous substance when they feel it. You bite it and the two substances, your thick saliva and the soft blood from his fingertip, mingle.

The contralto moans, and her lament turns you on. Could that intense, tormented voice resemble the voices of the nuns as they whip each other, or as they whip themselves?

It occurs to you because of her laments, because of that intense voice, because of her agonising moans, the agony of a wound or of a final spasm into your belly. You hold your lover's hand in both of yours, squeeze it hard, excited. You think again of the blood from Christ's side, the blood dripping down his face, his crown of thorns. The howls coming from Elektra, the dog, they hurt you, they wound your chest.

Applause interrupts your daydream. The singers leave with bunches of white flowers in their hands. You and your lover stand up from your seats and start clapping furiously.

PICTORIAL COPIES

You see him, tall, thin, with dark rings under his sad eyes and very long lashes; his hair is curly, his forehead high and his mouth well-defined, full yet delicate, his teeth very white; an olive skin tone; a long face with a cleft chin.

You admire his long, nervous hands, their long fingers, their short, pinkish nails; and his feet, like those of Christ in that Piero della Francesca in Arezzo.

You remember the scene:

Both of you in the enormous, old, solid oak bed right opposite the immense wardrobe with its bespoke, bevelled, almost old-fashioned mirror.

You sit up and move to the foot of the bed, check that you can see yourselves in the mirror, lean over and put his big toe in your mouth.

You return to the bed, stretch out, and he places the same toe, the one you brought to your mouth, inside your vagina. When you finish, you lean over his worked-up body again and kiss his perfect feet, identical in shape and colour to those of the Christ you saw in Arezzo.

Christ's feet are so beautiful, and even more so with Mary Magdalene washing them and drying them with her hair.

You always wished you could have been there, to die of that same disease.

LIKE DOGS

You are travelling constantly. Now you are in Italy, specifically Tarquinia, whose main attraction is the Etruscan frescos. You have already been to Pompeii, to the villas, the market, the brothel. The guide warned, when you looked at the paintings: 'ci sono qui qualche oscenità'.

You have seen them, you have seen Roman women making love like Lilith, like dogs, like modest matrons with their legs spread being ridden by men; or legs raised in incredible balancing acts; or hanging face down while the men stand. You have seen men performing fellatio; you have seen phalluses, fertility symbols, behind doors and bars, under lock and key; you have seen couples engrossed in their own pleasure being attended by servants; you have seen couples reaching orgasm while being observed; you have seen women sodomised by men armed with enormous instruments.

The frescos you are to visit in Tarquinia are held in a small room; a tomb.

—Ochre, you say, is the Etruscans' favourite colour.

One frieze has a border showing almost naked men on horseback, and others on foot in martial stances. The guide points to a spot on the wall and once again warns: 'qui si trovano anche qualche oscenità'.

You look carefully, about to make a comment about the ochre couple drawn on the wall. The guide, a slender, attractive Roman youth, turns towards your lover and they exchange a brief look that brings a familiar memory to mind. It's almost an obscene wink.

The fresco depicts two figures making love; one man is on all fours, his body an intense ochre; on top of him is a second man, in a paler ochre hue, squeezing his hind legs tightly around the body on which he is mounted.

YOU TREMBLE

You say:

—I don't believe it. I'm already dead. So why am I in so much pain?

You say this because, in truth, what is killing you is the desire to annihilate him.

Or – why not? – fury or jealousy.

Harassed, exhausted, you ask for my help.

There is nothing I can do, only look at you.

I break the silence to say:

—Remember, dogs – and bitches – also bite.

You reply, as always:

—Don't worry, all this is nothing but melodrama!

THE HAIR SHIRT

You wait for winter.

The messy house is killing you. Chairs in the middle of the room, half-upholstered, half-sanded furniture whose naked grain shows through clumsy layers of varnish: rosewood turned ebony through the magical work of dyes.

You find the havoc threatening. You sprawl on the floor, exhausted, repeating the ritual gesture of kings and queens in Elizabethan tragedies, a gesture signalling that all is lost. Men and women throw themselves to the ground, following the rhythm of life's wheel of fortune; they are knocked down, unequivocal sign of reality; it is impossible to fall any further, for you have to touch the ground if you are to hit rock bottom.

On the floor now, unable to exert the slightest effort, you let tears stream down your cheeks. You remember those long days by the sea, the delicious salty taste of it.

You return to the mess, the memories among the paintings, the scattered, half-sanded furniture, that rustic furniture stubbornly revealing different layers of dyes, hiding its beautiful old grain underneath.

You are still on the floor, alone among the objects. You imitate, with misplaced malice, those kings and queens fulfilling theatrical convention by rolling around on the floor, a sign of their acceptance of Fortune's designs. You are half-dressed, your hair uncombed, your face un-made-up, wearing only a black taffeta slip and your pointy, fine suede shoes.

Alone, completely alone. The girl has left.

You are reliving that scene. You lie on the floor in your underwear, remembering that you were getting ready in front of the mirror, wearing your suspender belt and stockings, leaving clear prints on the bathroom tiles. You can see it clearly: the mess and the half-finished chairs are a clear sign that it is impossible to make comparisons, to compare yourself with the grain of solid, old wood, much more solid than your own flesh, or than the story of your life.

You are still lying on the floor. You try to fix things, to break out of the cycle and get up, to use an artisanal procedure: to thin, strip, scrape off. Is it possible to recover the old grain of the wooden furniture, obscured by layers of dye? Is it possible to apply a similar process to all things, a process involving sandpaper, solvents and patience? Perhaps those marks, those acts of violence, can be erased in the same way that – through a complicated process of restoration – they managed to return the young woman to her portrait?

Something that speaks of loss, of destruction, of the disappearance of things, doesn't speak of itself, it speaks of others. Will it include them too?

Perhaps we shouldn't worry too much if the bodies of objects reveal the same frenzied violence – in their worn-out brocade and layers of varnish – as the body of Sister Lugarda de la Encarnación after the flagellation, the hair shirts, the fasting.

YOU WEEP

You talk to yourself, out loud, remembering the film. You say:

—I am overflowing with his absence. I am myself again, without him.

—Pure melodrama, I tell you.

You are quiet. You pay me no attention, then start weeping again:

—I'm not myself without you…
—I'm no longer myself without you…
—I cannot live without you, I cannot live with you… Not with you, nor without you…

You have his image in your body, your body overflows; half-submerged, almost weightless, you float; your riverbed is full to the brim.

You are quiet.

You speak up again:

—My name is no longer my name…

—How can I live without a heart? Outside, all the dogs urinate, it's what they do.

You know I am making fun of you, you know that weeping solves nothing, you know that you have fallen back into melodrama.

SHE GLANCES IN

You come out of your room and see her. The girl with the blue trousers is walking down the corridor. She arrives at the bathroom where the door is ajar, glances in and sees him naked in the tub, taking his morning bath. Something disturbs her; she turns away and hurries on. She is twelve.

The man in the bath has a curly, dark brown pubis.

HIS SHAPE HAS CHANGED

The dog has been shaved all over. He was suffering from a horrible infection. He looks like a different creature, his shape has changed, he is a shadow of himself. His skin is visible and a thick, silky, light black fluff is all that is left of his previous dark brown fur.

You play with him and he jumps up, excited, his enormous member impossible to ignore on that gaunt, diminished body, emerging like a kind of red intestine: it reminds you, though it's a different colour and consistency, of the recorder played at that concert you and your lover went to with the girl.

You imagine him mounting a female dog, as usual, except bald now. Obscene.

A FAINT THREAD OF A VOICE

In each other's arms on the bed, entirely naked, with the lights on, the two of you are about to make love.

He kisses you on the mouth, sticks his tongue between your teeth, and you bite it hard, making his tongue bleed.

He runs his tongue over your body, you feel him run it over your stomach, feel him push it into your vagina.

He straightens, takes your breast in his fingers and bites your right nipple. It stings, there is blood. You cry out.

He pulls his mouth away and you sit up and look at the drop of blood darkening the areola.

You tremble again when he flicks his tongue over it and licks the blood away.

He is about to enter you. You realise at that moment that there is a faint shaft of light, contrasting with the bright light of your room, coming in from the door. It is ajar; you know, you are sure, that you left it closed.

—It's her, you murmur, it's her!

The girl has been watching you noiselessly, without a word.

Distressed, you ask very quietly:

—How long has she been there?

—What did she see?

LAMB OF GOD

To protect them from sin and keep the nuns from temptation, animals have been banned from Lugarda's convent, especially dogs and cats.

As I write, Teresa Juana is whipping her sister with the same strength and consistency with which she flagellates her every morning. Something suddenly catches her attention: she has heard noises in the garden, but the rhythm with which she is beating Lugarda does not falter. Suddenly, another sound, a gasp; she turns, looks out of the cell window, thinks she can make out a shape moving. The whip falls from her hand. Lugarda's habit remains open to her waist and her wounds are leaking fresh blood. Teresa Juana looks closely: she sees a pair of dogs mating.

She backs away quickly from the window, returns to her place, crosses herself devoutly, picks up the whip and goes back to beating Lugarda de la Encarnación with awe-inspiring rhythm. The nun can no longer contain her moans, which quickly transform into screams as fresh blood runs down her back, staining her clothes. Teresa Juana moans too, the whip seeming to mark time.

She is silent. She does not stop, but goes on with the exercise, her voice breaking as she utters a prayer. I accompany her, writing it down:

—*Husband of mine!*

—*Sweet Jesus,*

—*Loving Master,*

—*Sweetest Jesus,*
—*Divine love,*
—*Beloved Lord, Blessed Sacrament.*
—*When will your beautiful light clothe my senses in glory?*
—*King of the heavens and of the earth,*
—*Immaculate lamb,*
—*Supreme goodness of all good things,*
—*Save me, Lord, lead me not into temptation.*
—*Deliver me from all evil...*
—*And drive the Devil far from us!*

Lugarda turns, facing her with her breasts bared. Tesera Juana continues to discipline her, barely looking at her. Then suddenly she stops and examines Lugarda carefully, her eyes passing quickly over her breasts, one of them round and white with nothing disturbing its smooth nakedness, its spherical shape; the other, like most breasts, has a rough areola and a very pink nipple. She catches her breath, directing the whip at her sister and starts hitting her slowly, rhythmically, alternating the blows from one breast to the other; she quickens the rhythm, now beating furiously without alternating sides, whipping only the smooth, white breast over and over again until the blood forms an areola. She has now left both breasts darkened and rough.

DELICATELY

You come in and sit at the table. When you are about to start serving the food, you see the girl enter with her white shirt, her blue trousers and a vase full of lilies and baby's breath. She places it on the sideboard, then she sits down the way he likes, knees together.

You serve the soup and she puts the spoon in her mouth delicately, without slurping. You serve the meat and she uses her knife and fork properly, chews with her mouth closed, silently, without putting her elbows on the table.

Your lover opens a bottle of wine with the red bottle opener.

—How lovely! cries the girl, spreading her legs as the cork comes out.

THEY DO NOT NEED FOOD

The nuns do not need food; it is enough for them to take communion. I write this phrase without hesitation. Didn't Saint Bernard say that the sacrament of the Eucharist could be compared with the process of eating human food? And to make this comparison tangible, he used similes of chewing, swallowing, assimilating and digesting.

(Simple, humble spirits will never be offended by simple things).

HER GREEDY THIRST

Lugarda does not eat, she does not eat common food, she cannot always digest it, but she is in the habit, out of love for her Husband, of ingesting abject, nauseating things. Her Husband rewards her; her Husband says:

—My beloved, your love for me has passed many tests. You have renounced all the pleasures of the body, gone to great lengths. Have you not taken the intensity of your love for me too

far? Have you not abolished even the most instinctive reflexes of your body? You have forced yourself to swallow what nature on principle rejects. I wish to reward you, to offer you a drink that, in its perfection, transcends everything produced in nature.

And taking her tenderly in his arms, he brought her close to his wound, the wound in his side.

—Drink, my beloved, drink, bring your lips to my wound, and by drinking my blood your soul will experience such great rapture that even your body, which you have renounced for my sake, will participate in your ecstasy.

Lugarda and Christ now form a single body. The nun drinks the delicious, thick, crimson liquid delightedly, and her bodily lips, cleaved to the wound, become celestial.

The seed of her destruction lies in that greedy thirst, that all-encompassing sensation, devastating.

A CERTAIN CADENCE

You are listening to music by Purcell, the same Ode to Saint Cecilia you always listen to. One of the fragments incites desire in you, the desire to hear a certain phrase again, a certain voice, a certain cadence: you rewind the disk and the concentrated sounds synthesise and deform the music, making it more perfect, and its maximum perfection is the fact that it has outlasted its time; Purcell would never have been able to hear himself synthesised like this, the chords so quick, the voices overlapping, the choruses uneven, unprecedented, unexpected. And they make you want to listen to Monteverdi next, to Ariadne's lament, a profane aria about ill-fated love, sung later, with the same music but different words, this time a sacred version, to express the lament of the sorrowful Virgin, her back to her Son, crucified, bloodstained. It is a scream, a howl, an irrational cry in its pure state, perfectly articulated, expressed as polished, harmonious chords, and yet, despite it all, distilled into a cry, a shriek, thanks to the voice of a mezzosoprano trained to modulate, according to ideals, a mythical lament, the incomparable essence of pain, the pain of absence, the pain of love.

And that voice, you think again, that raw yet harmonised lament, deepens the experience of waiting and connects you to the silence of a device that can contain other voices: it charts that strange link between the telephone line and an intense love affair about to be cut off.

A perpetual obsession, the search for that beloved man on the other end of the line while feeling Ariadne's cry in your gut.

THE SHADOW OF HIS MOUTH

The light flickers and changes hue as it passes through the different coloured reflectors. Some of the normal lights, by the columns, have cheap imitations of art deco lampshades and the one beside you is blinding: it is broken and the bulb is bare. The dancefloor is packed; everyone is dancing to the rhythm of an orchestra made up of very dark-skinned men, dressed without exception as though they were somewhere hot and tropical, despite the fact it is winter and cold out. Their trousers and shoes are white, their shirts are short-sleeved, made of cheap, shiny, clashing fabrics. As they play, they mark the rhythm with their feet and hips, following the dancers on the dancefloor.

You are dancing too, pressed against your lover, right up against him. He passes both hands around your waist, drops one to your hip, then caresses your back. Your bodies form a unit, and the music is as loud and violent as the shirts of the men who are playing it.

You look up and around. Everyone is dancing, just like you, the same ecstatic, sensual expression on all their faces.

The couples could be interchangeable: the same chubby, greasy bodies, no waists, protruding bellies, short legs and inelegant faces, and on top of all that, clothes fitted proudly to all their protuberances.

You sit down and fix your gaze on the dancers: all the bodies, whether deformed or svelte, are moving gracefully, always elastic, always redeemed by sensuality. A tall Black man dressed entirely in white is dancing with a slight, very attractive, brown-skinned girl. The man's overhanging belly fits perfectly into her torso. They dance, knowing how to alternate between contracting the muscles of their backs and then their shoulders; their feet slowly mark the beat, their motionless hips emphasising the elegant rhythm marked out by the muscles of their upper bodies. The man's hand traps the girl's waist, touching it gently to set her rhythm with a joyful confidence: they are haughty, magnificent, almost perverse.

The music ceases; the couples abandon the floor. The singer appears in a traje de luces, one plump, white, translucent shoulder bare except for a covering of silver leaves, perfect partner to an enormous flower on her imposing chest, like a mountain range above her considerable belly. She has no waist and her hips form uneven rolls illuminated suddenly by the spotlights; her very high heels – open-toed platforms with an ankle strap – reveal ruddy strips of solid white flesh, creating a perfect symmetry with her shoulders.

Other singers come to mind, now, opera singers. A stocky, regal woman wearing a short-sleeved, black tulle gown, her chest covered with black sequins that flash furiously in the stage lighting; her mouth is wide, large, clearly outlined and seemingly duplicated by another, paler mouth where the play of her voice and the coloratura of each of her registers are reproduced with greater force. The voice and its shadow fall on the mouth and its ghost. Behind her, a fat, bearded tenor exhales a superhuman cry in a pure, powerful voice, full of trills, rising again and again until it reaches the same melody an octave higher. Flashes of light illuminating his white teeth, making the sequins glitter on the chest of the soprano, who gradually increases the volume of her song. And now, in duet, both manage to reach the highest note singable by human voices, whose satiny softness expresses a sigh of love, the most delicate and tender ever to emerge from such elephantine throats.

The song you are listening to tonight is accompanied by electronic instruments and the woman's voice surpasses them; it is greater than her monumental, almost sacred body: there is no expression on her face as she sings, only sweat, dripping transparently down the rolls of her neck, as silky and shiny as the fabric of her gown.

Your table faces the men's bathroom. There is a violent promiscuity to the dance, the sweaty bodies, the food, the drink, the coming and going of the waiters and the opening and closing of the door that violently illuminates that small space that men are constantly entering, all dressed as though they were in the tropics, groping their women on the dancefloor and then, all squeezed together, each other in the bathroom.

The backslaps resound dryly, muffled by the fat they are carrying; they close the door except for a crack, and you can just make out, as though half-asleep, their satisfied faces and white teeth.

Your gaze shifts, you focus on the singer, then look at your lover. The woman sings, her contralto voice projecting, covering any imperfection with its sound, any distraction. Her hand movements become vicious, spiteful, and the flashing of her diamond bracelets underscores her rage, her thwarted love, her vengeful, degraded, degrading words. Concentrating grievances in his hand and rage in his nails, your lover reinscribes on your palm a wild and eloquent rancour.

YOU WOULD LIKE TO DO HER MAKE UP

The girl in the portrait intrigues you. You had stopped talking about her, but now you have taken up the topic again and for a few days have been returning to it constantly whenever we speak. Her slight smile intrigues you, her thin, pink lips, the ambiguous look in her make-up-free eyes.

Do you think it would be necessary to do her make-up? (Perhaps it would outline her gaze). Her clean face distresses you, her eyeliner-less eyes make you think about how they would look made-up (with mascara, eyeliner, eyeshadow, blusher, her hair wavy and cut short).

Those make-up-free eyes reveal a desire (like the desire of the girl lying on the sofa with her legs spread, in her blue trousers and white top?).

THE GIRL TELLS YOU

The girl tells you she has been going to Church. She tells you she goes to confession, confesses her sins, and that the priest gives her penance, though not much: twenty Hail Marys, ten Creeds, fifteen Our Fathers. She prays them quickly and then joins the queue to take communion: she feels the host slip between her teeth, over her tongue, its long, tight, choking journey down her throat. Her heart, she tells you, starts burning and the Christ Child is rocked inside her, right there, deep within her chest.

She feels agile, perfect, she adds. She goes to the cinema and her friends are waiting for her outside. They too have confessed and taken communion. She likes these girls, five years older than her, much wiser, more confident, wearing the same clothes, blue trousers and a white shirt.

In the cinema she sits very carefully, she explains, legs together, like a lady. Her friends buy sweets and she accepts some from them. When she chews, she hears a loud noise as they come apart, crunchy and sugary, on her tongue.

Having taken communion, she remembers the Baby Jesus sitting inside her chest and is sorry to have disturbed him. Gently, discreetly, she drops the rest of the packet down the side of her seat. Her chest goes back to being that flowering meadow where the gentle Christ Child lies contented.

The girl gives you a bunch of carnations. She is wearing a red ribbon in her hair, her blonde, rosy-cheeked doll lying on the chair. The girl, too, has a tender, very pale down that caresses her cheeks.

You can see her transfiguring before your eyes. She is almost a teenager.

THE DIRTY, DARK RED MOUTH

The dog is about to give birth. You can tell by her movements, her restlessness. You are worried, and go over to where she's lying. You see her moving, unpleasantly, as she lies panting where her labour has begun. Will it be like all births? Will the amniotic fluid be salty? You cannot answer these questions, a puppy is now being born, sticky blood gushing, spilling onto the box, soaking the newspapers, a bright red colour that soon forms a little black puddle. The thickness of the blood, the brownish colour of the placenta and other excrescences make you feel sick.

The dog licks her own blood, then stops. You watch her, her snout a dirty, dark red colour. The newspapers are soaked through too. Another puppy is born and the dog lunges for the placenta, whose shape repels you, but you overcome your disgust and take it from her to stop her from eating it. You examine the new-born dog with its fur stuck to its body, but you don't dare touch it. It completely repulses you, almost making you vomit, and yet you are moved, touched: soft, short, sticky fur swirls over the little bloodstained body, highlighting the animal's vulnerability. Suddenly it gets up, legs trembling, and begins to walk, soaking wet, testing out its strength. You stop it, cut the umbilical cord with the scissors, see the blood run, see and feel your sticky fingers, and nausea rises up your throat; at that precise moment the mother lets out a brief howl and you see the head of another animal emerging. There is barely time for you to catch it in your arms. Everything surrounding the dog is soaked; you don't know how you have held it together. One of the puppies is male and it too has curly, sticky fur, which the mother starts licking, cleaning with her tongue, but the puppy slips away from her, gets up, and to your astonishment starts to walk, fast, faster, doing pirouettes, while the other one, lying down, wants only to suckle. You push away your disgust, take the puppy in your hands and examine it. It's a honey-coloured female with lighter patches on her back. Her tiny nipples are already visible, miniature versions of those on the belly of her mother, that obliging wet nurse, ready to feed them with her heavy teats, practically dragging along the floor, which the new-born female will share with the other puppies when they are born.

You examine the mother again, surmising that she will shortly give birth to another creature, here it is already, the head is emerging so you help it out, holding it, turning it, cutting the cord with the scissors. You flip it over to examine it and it's a female, dark brown like her father. You have overcome your repugnance, you have become a skilled example.

By the time it's over you are exhausted, pensive, dirty. You help the mother rest, arranging her in her basket and laying her puppies beside her. Once the labour is over, you wake the girl up so she can see them, help you clean them and wipe off the blood splattered all over you.

SHE FALLS

You've gone to get your nails painted in that bright colour you like. There are rings on your fingers and a thick silver bracelet over your dark jumper. The varnish is fresh, you have to make sure not to smudge it so its shiny surface remains smooth.

You turn on the machine and put on the album you like, listening to the trumpets. They start things off furiously, before the contralto comes in, or maybe it's the countertenor, or both, singing in duet. You raise your right hand and see long white marks on two of your nails, like a wound breaking through the scarlet colour you ritually choose.

The music resounds behind you; it's the trumpets' turn now, conversing with the countertenor, struggling to reach a high note that in other times was reserved for castrati. They say that in certain registers their voices were like those of sopranos, although its sound was simultaneously that of a woman and a fifteen-year-old boy, at that disturbing limit where the voice breaks, when it is on the point of defining itself, of breaking with ambiguity. And the incredibly high register culminates with a wild note of exaggerated sensuality: its cadence is magnificent, reiterated, rising higher and higher, without transitioning, dragging an immense sadness behind it.

Perhaps it's the final note, sung by the contralto who plays the role of Orpheus: he has disobeyed the gods, given into Eurydice's entreaties and looked at her; they are not yet out of Hell.

She falls. Orpheus cries out and his cry is superhuman.

You have understood: your lover is gradually disappearing from your world, abandoning you. Have you lost your body?

You cannot contain yourself. You cover your face with your hands. The bright, garish colour of your nails is visible. One of your rings dazzles me.

FACE UP

You sleep, lying on your back beside him. He sits up, gently lifts the sheet and looks at you, pausing on your breasts. They fit in his hands, he squeezes them. You move vaguely, turning over, and his hand gently traces the contours of your back and hip. You feel his caress like that of a mother: you have returned to infancy.

SHE LOOKS AT HERSELF IN THE MIRROR

It is night. You look in, the bed is unmade, but you can't see the girl in the room. You go in and straighten the sheets, which are flowery, beige and red, to match the towels in the bathroom. There is only one light, the bedside lamp.

The bedroom is strangely tidy. You call her but she does not reply. You go to look for her around the house, to order her to go to bed, she has school tomorrow. You cannot find her anywhere. Something suddenly tells you that she is back in her room.

You return. There she is. Naked except for a white bikini with little pink flowers on it. She is looking at herself in the mirror on her dressing table, everything strangely tidy, unusually so, her clothes hung up, colour coordinated, her white shirts next to her perfectly folded blue trousers, no toys or books strewn over the floor; there are cosmetics, powder, eyeshadows, eyeliners, and lipliners in an open drawer. The door is wide open and the lights are on. There is something strange about her face, something changed in her gaze, a peculiar gleam.

You understand, suddenly you understand: her lips are painted, there is eyeshadow on her eyes and her smile is vulgar – lewd?

THE BRUSH OF HIS HAND

The bed is wide, its curved wooden headrest a dark colour, highly varnished. The duvet, the pillows and the mattress are made of feathers. He appears to be asleep in the bed. You are sitting up and reading.

The girl tiptoes in, dressed as she always is, in blue trousers and a white shirt; she looks at you from the door, holding the nail clippers in her right hand, barefoot. She walks towards the bed and when she gets to where he is sleeping, she bends down until her face is level with his.

Then he opens his eyes.

—What do you want? he asks.

—For you to cut my nails, she answers, and holds the clippers out to him.

—Get in the bed, he orders.

And the girl does so, falling like a cloud, softly, the blades of the clippers above her face. He is frozen, not even blinking, then snaps out of it, lifts the duvet, leans forward, places a palm on the sole of her foot, lightly separates the girl's dirty toes and, one by one, gently cuts her nails.

They fall soft and white on the bed: a happy smile brightens the girl's eyes.

A SPARK

*L*ugarda *hears her sister, she hears her talking about her visions, visions that I will record here:*

—*I have seen,* Juana *says, a little spark of divine fire.*

She understands fully that this is a mercy granted her by heaven and that she has received yet another mercy from her Beloved: Juana *tells of how she was, on one occasion, taken into his presence, and how the Lord, drawing him to her with the most loving caresses, began to indulge himself with her, passing his divine hands over her cheeks and face, and as though that were not enough for her to understand how much he loved her, he said, with such extreme tenderness:*

—*My daughter, console yourself, accept my caresses, for they are a sign that all your sins will be forgiven.*

Juana *never forgot those words, and in order not to forget them, she went on with her exercises and prayers, devout and unceasing. Lugarda could not forget them either, and imitating* Juana, *prayed and did her penance with great fervour.*

—*O what beautiful hands!* Juana *remembers.*

—*O what words! Lugarda de la Encarnación adds.*

—*I must continue in my labours,* Teresa Juana *insists, even if it costs me my life!*

And visions came to them often, and when they did, they recounted them, gathered with their other sisters during the convent's common services.

They did not see the Eucharistic species, the divine bread did not appear to them, but Christ himself did. He tended to reveal himself as an extremely beautiful child of five or six; at other times they venerated him at his most perfect age, with the same appearance and clothing with which he lived in the world. A simple, immense brightness would appear suddenly before their eyes, interrupted by other strange, rare and delicate gifts, which caused them to spend those days so enraptured and ecstatic that they provoked general astonishment.

Someone told me that when God granted them these gifts they would burst into gorgeous song, full of such tender affection and sung with such honest elegance, such pure phrasing, in such resonant voices and such a variety of chords that, venerating their voices as they venerated heaven, the other nuns were left silent and enraptured, sharing in their visions.

THE HEAVILY MADE-UP FACE

You pass by there often, alone. This time your lover is driving; the girl is in the back, lying down, her legs up on the seats, dressed as always in her blue trousers and white shirt. There are two acrobats on the corner, a couple.

The man is old, dressed as a clown in a clown's predictably enormous black shoes. He is holding a little girl by the hand, a girl around five years old with a heavily made-up face, her lips and nose stretched grotesquely into a clown's leer that is contradicted by her clean eyes and brows: her gaze is absent, inexpressive. A brightly coloured, disproportionately large shirt hangs off her body, along with very baggy trousers; enormous balloons stuffed down the back give her a grotesque gait. The man holding her hand, and whom she follows obediently, pulls obscene faces at the other homeless people on the corner.

You are motionless; your lover watches them, indifferent. You turn around, observe the girl out of the corner of your eye. Her face is expressionless, but she has spread her legs even wider.

IF THERE IS LOVE

You know, you have always had a tenderness, a gift that is neither entirely sensual nor entirely spiritual. If there is love, there are also tears. Sometimes it seems like you're crying on purpose, other times like you can't help yourself.

You know this comparison offering itself to you is full of joy and that this feeling tends to present itself at ungodly hours, the feeling of his presence, making you feel certain he is there, and, though you can't see him, remembering him is enough for you to experience pleasure as though his body were present.

You see him inside your chest, a perfect image. You seek him in every corporeal nature, in every earthly nature, you find his substance in your own soul, you see it, you know it is invisible, but always corporeal.

Since we are carnal, it must be that our desire and our love shall have its beginning in the flesh.

—Isn't that how pleasure grows, uncontainably?

EVERYTHING IS CLEARER

He starts drinking champagne and reading his favourite poems aloud.

He leans forward and offers you some; you wet your lips.

He puts the book down, turns on the record player, and you hear the voice of an actor reading the same poems he has been reciting.

You stretch out on the floor and he lies next to you. The actor's voice is monotonous, agreeable, beautiful.

He takes the glass and drenches you, bubbles tickling; he leans over and kisses your breasts, bites a nipple gently, runs his tongue over your wide areola, and as he licks your rough, bumpy skin, you feel him savour the bittersweet taste of champagne.

You have the feeling of being propelled upwards, rising, rising, hearing confused words murmured behind you.

You stop listening to them.

Everything is clearer, as clear as can be, a blinding light now, the actor's voice cutting through you, warming your heart, softening you.

Or is it that he is breathing so close to you that it is making your eyes blur?

FROM ONE MOUTH TO THE OTHER

Juana suddenly starts chewing the holy bread. She mashes it between her teeth and then removes the pieces from her mouth. She opens Lugarda's mouth and gently inserts them one by one.

Sister Lugarda mashes them between her teeth and then lines her face up with that of her sister —her sister in faith, or her real sister? She kisses her and immediately feels great consolation, a great sweetness flooding her, a feeling of supreme wellbeing flowing from one mouth to the other.

Then she realises that nothing, no other consolation, no other tenderness could surpass that feeling. And that sense of peace lasts for days, days during which Juana and Lugarda weep steadily, sunk in an inexplicable silence.

VERY SUDDENLY

You are sitting in front of the mirror. You are wearing a black and white outfit made from fine wool, a full, black, lightly-pleated skirt and a turquoise belt, cinched tight: your white blouse contrasts with the black bolero you have thrown over your shoulders. You look at yourself in delight. You are like a portrait, a portrait of a teenager in the mirror.

Suddenly, to your surprise, the girl is in your bed.

—Is it her? you ask me.

When you get up to look at the image, your breasts stand out. You are duplicated, the other image appearing behind you.

—Can't you see her? I ask.

You point to her and repeat:

—The girl, she's there.

—In front of the mirror, on the bed, like the young woman who reappears in the portrait?

She is dozing innocently, her hair tied back in plaits. She stretches out her left hand and some of her fingers bend gently as she places her ring finger near her mouth; her other arm is raised too, and her white shirt reveals part of her torso. Her breasts are round, small. From the waist down she is naked; her legs are spread wide; her pubic hair is ash-blonde, almost white, transparent. You can see her opening, her labia offering themselves up to your gaze, delicate, pink, soft.

You open your eyes when you hear footsteps, which stop by the half-open door; she has heard them too: she immediately inserts her right index finger into her vagina and starts to masturbate at a constant, uniform rhythm. Her orgasm comes very suddenly.

The girl opens her mouth in ecstasy, letting her wet

tongue push out between her teeth: it is an intense, bright colour. She then places the finger she has masturbated with in her mouth and sucks it in delight.

The image disappears suddenly, and you are left alone in front of the mirror.

THE VISIONS

As I write her, I hear her say aloud words that have come to her from heaven.

—Have faith, my daughter, and you will receive sacred food. If you suffer for my sake, I will be your consolation. I am in you, you venerate me and in return for your love and your pain you will receive that which you desire. Have faith, my daughter, stay close to your sister, Lugarda, unite yourself with her, so that from her mouth my breath may pass into yours.

Juana obeyed and Lugarda bled into her mouth. And that instant was no different from the sacrament in mass, when the priest drinks from the Holy Chalice, or when he delivers the Spiritual Food to those who wish to commune with God.

And then Juana Teresa de Cristo said:

—The sweet taste of Divine Grace has entered me and my inner being is illuminated and is witness to the miraculous visions that the handmaid of the Lord, my sister in faith, Lugarda de la Encarnación, has experienced. You are right to call me! You are right that I am yours!

In the visions they enjoyed a delicious holy banquet, God's banquet, served and officiated by the handmaid of the Lord. There they met the Most Holy Trinity in unity of essence, as when mass is celebrated.

Since then, the two sisters have looked at each other in the mirror and divine understanding has dawned in them too. Their perception is sharp as steel, sharp as the lance that pierces his side. That is why they collide, cut, penetrate, discover the truth; they read each other's minds, know what the other feels, utter the same burning words addressed to Him, feel his pain together, share the same state of mind, as if their own blood were being spilled. What one feels, the other can surmise, their thoughts are shaken, provoked, and their minds return to the hair shirts, the fasting, the flagellations.

Thanks to the blood that one has spilt in the mouth of the other, Teresa Juana is Lugarda and Lugarda Teresa Juana.

RINGS ON YOUR FINGERS

You sit down, spread your legs wide. Your labia part and your clitoris emerges. You place one of your fingers between your legs and begin to move it, then lift your other arm and with your other hand, the left hand, stroke your nipples, first one and then the other, rubbing them systematically, making sure the two rhythms are in sync. Your labia swell, you are approaching orgasm, you pause…

You lie on the floor on the cold tiles, close your legs, position your hands as you want them again, cross them over your body, push your finger between your labia and with the other hand, the one that has rings on every finger, take your nipple and squeeze it hard.

You change hands; now it's your left hand, the one with only one ring on the index finger. You put your finger between your labia, lie back. You are in front of the mirror, studying your reactions, the stone of the ring reflecting brightly. You are turned on, you pick up the rhythm again until you feel simultaneous pain and pleasure.

—Did you enjoy that?

You put your index finger in your mouth, savouring the delicious salty taste and reply:

—No. I miss him.

MY ONLY TORMENT

As he and I drifted apart, as our separation became more marked, Lugarda decided to do harder penance. With the help of her sister, Teresa Juana, she properly set out on her path to sainthood. In place of the delicate Dutch linen she had worn, she made a tunic, a kind of shirt, out of serge, removed her mattress and chose sheets whose little wrinkles hurt her body, and slept on nothing but two thin planks with no headrest at all, wearing no nightclothes except a thin blanket with which she covered her body so as not to leave it naked. Around her arms, thighs, and waist she tied a belt made from horsehair and steel chains, and she covered her breasts and back with uneven stripes. She would put a handful of pebbles in her shoes, or (horrifying to think) sometimes even a scattering of sharp nails.

She was not content with what the rules dictated and so practised other, more rigorous disciplines, and when she was too ill or in pain for these, her cruel sister would begin to shout angrily, her sister who, taking up her discipline, rained countless lashes down on her (and, as far as I can see, did so entirely guiltlessly, because the aim was to make her sister saintly, which she apparently desired). In the face of these and other, perhaps more sensitive, exercises sometimes inflicted on her, Mother Lugarda always showed respectful patience and a serene countenance.

Sometimes she would sigh:

—This sister of mine is my only torment, a dark shadow that robs me of sunlight.

The lashes on her back formed bloody lines, curious arabesques on her body. Teresa Juana took fervent care that Lugarda's wounds were always fresh, and would sometimes sing psalms as she cracked the whip:
—O, it throbs, it burns, it bleeds, o, sister, thank you for allowing me to help you carry your cross!

THE PLAYERS

It's late, the party has tired you out. So many vague, similar faces: banal, repetitive, circular conversations. You move among them offering drinks or canapés to lighten the burden and avoid useless comments. You are fed up, tired. The girl circulates in her perpetual outfit, her blue trousers and white shirt; her mocking eyes show the pleasure she takes in noting your helplessness and boredom. The dogs circulate among the guests, wagging their tails, sometimes tripping people up; you call to them, stroke them. It's been a while now since you gave away the puppies.

He circulates with his glass of whisky in hand without even trying it; he stops from time to time to say something, something wonderful, you deduce, judging by the rapt faces of the pale guests. Their clothes are shameful; you compare their bright, multicoloured shirts, covered in slogans – where you can read, infinitely slowly, their ungainly minds – with the girl's white shirt; they are wearing the exact same trousers as her, but look dreadful in them.

You are suffocating, you think you are going to faint; a wave of nausea compels you to go to the toilet. Once you are there, the nausea passes; instead, an immense, uncontrollable wave of rage shakes you. An acrid taste in the mouth, like the smell of concentrated urea; your saliva is thick, sticky, it contains an acid that protects your teeth from pain, as though it were made of clove extract, but it tastes like poison. Nausea again, intense as an orgasm.

You are still shut away, trying to contain the rage coursing through your entire body, first your stomach, then your chest and finally your corrupted mouth.

You do not come out until the noise of the house quietens. You hear the girl's footsteps and the sound of her door closing. You hear his footsteps heading towards the bedroom. You wait a few seconds then emerge and head towards your bedroom. Again you feel spasms of rage coursing through each of your innards; you try to contain yourself but know ahead of time that you are going to explode.

You go in.

You are surprised to see he is already wearing his pyjamas. You are surprised by how closely you examine all the fabric's tiniest details. You see his slippers and the immense bed where they have been asleep without touching one another for some time. He reproaches you, sarcastic, hurtful. You do not reply, choked with rage. He speaks again, makes an even more unpleasant comment. You can no longer contain yourself. You launch yourself at him. You hit him in the face, tearing the thin, arabesque-patterned fabric, you scrape your nails down his back, running them freely over his bare skin. You know it will bleed and that your scratches will sting.

He says something else, something very offensive, in an almost inaudible voice. You take off your shoes and scratch him again with a sharp heel, leaving a deeper, long, red mark.

He is motionless, tears running down his cheeks. You see them and another wave of impotent rage shakes you even more violently. You know the girl has noticed nothing; the scene has taken place in the most ominous silence.

THE SAME CRY

The voice pierces you, the high-pitched cry of a soprano, a lament, and the same cry resounds inside you. It is a white lance.

It's off-key, all the better to pierce you with.

THE WEDDING

You are on your way to the village, to a wedding, the wedding of a relative. He is driving, you are sitting beside him, the girl is in the back with her legs comfortably stretched out across the seats.

You and the girl are dressed up, the girl in a new tailored outfit that shows off her very small round breasts, her narrow hips. The neckline of her dress reveals her long, thin neck, her fragile, graceful, innocent neck. She has the skin of a baby and still exhales a childlike, unpolluted smell.

He does not speak. His hostility weighs heavy on the atmosphere. You think of the red tracks down his back, of the cruelty of your crimson nails, and glance at your hands full of rings.

The girl is humming a popular song, and you realise the tension is growing, intensifying; you note his hands gripping the wheel and remember other fights, the petty, dishonest, useless, defiant words, yours, your daughter's, his, and the anger that reddens your faces; you remember how one day he slapped her, remember your reaction and the horrendous things you said to him. You remember how he got up and left, closing the door behind him, remember thinking you would never see him again. Yet the three of you are there, sitting in the car, all dressed up, too elegant, you and the girl, inadequate.

The place is beautiful, ancient, full of old monuments; the morning is sunny and the sky is clear. The girl meets her friends, dressed as she is with an elegance that is out of place, with the same thin, precocious little bodies. You are still together, you and he; someone offers you a glass, and the tension dissipates as you drink. A friendly conversation with other guests seems to calm the mood.

After the meal, there is dancing. You are in the middle of the countryside and the dancefloor is on uneven, rough, dusty ground. Your high heels sink into the dry mud. You start dancing with him, he pulls you close, the music is tropical, winding. You think of – you wish for – a possible reconciliation, of being alone with him, in bed, making love like before, without interruptions, with enormous passion. Or following his orders, on the floor on all fours.

Something is wrong, you realise suddenly, emerging from your reverie; you start focusing on the words he is whispering in your ear as he dances with you, holding you very tightly.

He begins to murmur right in your ear. You barely understand the words; he repeats them, gradually conveying them to your brain. You hear them, but you don't want to understand them, and in any case, the music keeps interrupting their flow. But he goes on, imperturbable, like a machine producing dissonant phrases, a broken record: you hear only loose words, intoned according to a convulsive, contemptuous rhythm.

He goes on whispering; his words burn, sting. His voice resounds like the trumpets, in a sharp, triumphal tone, much like the sound that emerges from the record you often listen to, the Purcell one, the Ode to Saint

Cecilia, glorious music, when the trumpets accompany the countertenor imitating the castrati. Didn't you have those explosive orgasms together? Triumphant orgasms, as sublime and lofty as those of the furious trumpet or the castrato hitting the high notes, lifted by a unique modulation, a clear, penetrating timbre, an octave higher than a natural female voice, which always reaches a dry, hard register, a voice that differs from a female voice and yet is brilliant, light, powerful. He is talking non-stop. Suddenly he falls quiet: your heart is already in pieces.

And then the rage again, that rage that resounds inside you like the wrath of God, tempered fury, the fury of the metal with which trumpets are made.

You stumble on the hard mud, your party shoes stuck in the clay, ruined, your tights ripped. The music is infernal, strident, making his words more violent, his breath hotter as he whispers in your ear; fury, and also increasing your immense desire to make love to him.

You stop, move away, and he immediately adopts a strange position. He holds his arms out in a cross shape and waits, as though he knows what you are going to do, as though he knows perfectly how you are going to react. Your hands pull away resentfully, letting them fall slowly to your sides; then finally, on an impulse, you slap him. The orchestra attacks the notes, hot, off-key, piercing. The slaps resound on his face, one after another, several times. He doesn't move, his arms held out in a cross shape and his gaze pleading, while tears run down your cheeks: there is nothing between you anymore. You look around you, everyone is dancing without paying you any attention. In the distance, standing in her party dress with her fragile little body, her shining eyes, the girl looks mockingly at you: an obscene, scornful smile plays on her lips.

MIRACLE OF MIRACLES

I sit at the keyboard, dressed in my severe, dark, grey and white checked suit, place the tips of my fingers on the keys, feel the pleasure of writing in my fingertips. I hurry, I want the vision to reappear for the last time.

Lugarda is praying on her knees, her back to me, her habit lowered to her waist, and Juana, scourge in hand, is whipping her at the serene, implacable pace of a mental metronome. On the wall opposite there is a life-sized image of the Christ on the Cross, who seems to be watching the scene as Lugarda returns his gaze with pained attention.

—Stop, she says to Juana.

She turns, takes Juana's hands, removes the scourge from them, frees herself; she arranges her habit a little and grazes her fresh wounds with a slight shiver; one of her breasts shows an erect nipple on its rough, darkened areola; the other, the right one, is still round, no bumps, no shape tarnishing the perfect sphere of white flesh.

She stands as though on a cross, looking at her divine Husband, accompanying him as she meditates on the pain, agony, neglect and death he suffered on the Cross. She feels the same torments in her soul, wants to feel the same torments in her body.

She picks up the scourge she had left on the floor. Juana moves away. Lugarda whips herself over and over again, many times; she is entirely covered in blood, her back, her chest; she stops, pauses, and then whips herself again, directing her discipline to her breasts, striking the white, smooth breast again and again, increasing the force and accelerating the rhythm until the blood forms an areola on her white breast. Her two breasts are now darkened and rough.

Alternating with Juana, Lugarda says:

—Husband of mine,

—Sweet Jesus,
—Loving Master,
—Sweetest Jesus,
—Divine love,
—Beloved Lord, Blessed Sacrament,
—When will your beautiful light clothe my senses in glory?
—King of heaven and earth,
—Immaculate lamb,
—Supreme goodness of all good things,
—Miracle of miracles!

In that instant, the Lord calls her, takes her by the hand and places his crown on her head. He enters her, penetrating the most intimate part of her heart and soul. They are so united and identical that a single Cross, a handful of nails and a crown crucifies them both, Christ, Lugarda, Incarnate.

She cries out in pain:

—But —o glory!— when will I ever deserve to enjoy your serene light?

And suddenly she, Sister Lugarda, appears mounted on the statue, her feet and hands nailed to the Cross, her entire being imprinted on Christ and Christ portrayed in her. Lugarda's body hides the image of the Lord: the divine haloed head appears to recline on that of the nun, her head also crowned with thorns.

Sister Juana Teresa prays a psalm:

O my, what joy! Sweet nails that have crucified my beloved, fix me to the Cross so that I may die with Him.

ACKNOWLEDGMENTS

My thanks go to Pier Paolo Pasolini, Kawabata, Georges Bataille, Teresa de Jesús, Juana Inés de la Cruz, Tanizaki, Roland Barthes, Sigüenza y Góngora, Akutagawa, Giorgio de Chirico, Carolyn Walker Bynum, María Ignacia, Margaret King, Agustín de la Madre de Dios, José Gorostiza, Ignacio de Loyola, Catarina de Siena, Fumiko Enchi, Marguerite Duras, Carlo Ginzburg, Inés de la Cruz, Francisco de la Maza, Oviedo Francisco Frías and Catarina de San Juan, authors whose texts I have used, sometimes, quite literally. I am grateful to Pilar Ferragut and Turina Oliveira for their kind help. Finally, I'd like to reiterate my thanks to Kawabata, Diamela, Luz, and Beatriz; and, last but not least, I must mention G.M., L.F., H.J and M.S.D.

About the Author

Margo Glantz fused Yiddish literature, Mexican culture, and French tradition to create experimental new works of literature. Glanz graduated from the National Autonomous University of Mexico (UNAM) in 1953 and earned a doctorate in Hispanic literature from the Sorbonne in Paris before returning to Mexico to teach literature and theater history at UNAM. A prolific essayist, she is best known for her 1987 autobiography *Las genealogías* (The Genealogies), which blended her experiences of growing up Jewish in Catholic Mexico with her parents' immigrant experiences. She also wrote fiction and nonfiction that shed new light on the seventeenth-century nun Sor Juana Inés de la Cruz. Among her many honours, she won the Magda Donato Prize for *Las genealogías* and received a Rockefeller Grant (1996) and a Guggenheim Fellowship (1998).

She has been awarded honorary doctorates from the Universidad Autónoma Metropolitana (2005), the Universidad Autónoma de Nuevo León (2010), and the Universidad Nacional Autónoma de México (2011). Glantz was awarded the 2004 National Prize for Sciences and the prestigious FIL Prize in 2010. She received Chile's Manuel Rojas Ibero-American Narrative Award in 2015.

About the Translator

Ellen Jones is a writer, editor, and translator from Spanish. Her recent translations include *Beyond Mestizaje: Contemporary Debates on Race in Mexico* edited by Tania Islas Weinstein and Milena Ang (2024), *Cubanthropy* by Iván de la Nuez (2023) and *The Remains* by Margo Glantz (shortlisted for the Warwick Prize for Women in Translation 2023). Her monograph, *Literature in Motion: Translating Multilingualism Across the Americas* is published by Columbia University Press (2022). Her short fiction has appeared in *Litro Magazine*, *Slug* and *The London Magazine*.

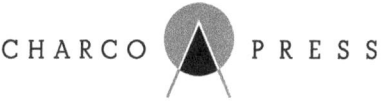

Director & Editor: Carolina Orloff
Director: Samuel McDowell

www.charcopress.com

The text was designed using Bembo 11.5 and ITC Galliard.

www.ingramcontent.com/pod-product-compliance
Lightning Source LLC
Jackson TN
JSHW021159140326
99318JS00003B/363